bad blood

bad blood

DEMITRIA LUNETTA

Delacorte Press

Text copyright © 2017 by Demitria Lunetta
Jacket photographs: figure © 2016 by Irene Lamprakou/Arcangel,
background © by Superstock
Jacket design by Mark Swen

All rights reserved. Published in the United States by Delacorte Press, an imprint of Random
House Children's Books, a division of Penguin Random House LLC, New York.

Delacorte Press is a registered trademark and the colophon is a trademark
of Penguin Random House LLC.

randomhouseteens.com

Educators and librarians, for a variety of teaching tools, visit us at RHTeachersLibrarians.com

Library of Congress Cataloging-in-Publication Data.
Names: Lunetta, Demitria, author.
Title: Bad blood / Demitria Lunetta.
Description: First edition. | New York : Delacorte Press, [2017] |
Summary: Spending her summer vacation with her aunt, who lives in Edinburgh, Scotland,
sixteen-year-old Heather MacNair is haunted by dreams and compelled to cut herself until
she discovers a family secret and a past full of magic that could both save her and put her in
mortal danger.
Identifiers: LCCN 2016009266 | ISBN 978-1-101-93805-8 (hc) |
ISBN 978-1-101-93807-2 (ebook)
Subjects: | CYAC: Families—Fiction. | Magic—Fiction. | Cutting (Self-mutilation)—Fiction. |
Edinburgh (Scotland)—Fiction. | Scotland—Fiction.
Classification: LCC PZ7.L9791155 Bad 2017 | DDC [Fic]—dc23

The text of this book is set in 12-point Garamond.
Interior design by Ken Crossland

Printed in the United States of America
10 9 8 7 6 5 4 3 2 1

First Edition

Random House Children's Books supports the First Amendment
and celebrates the right to read.

bad blood

1
primrose

June 13, 1629
Edinburgh, Scotland

BLACK SMOKE SCALDS my lungs.

A crowd is gathered, their faces lit by the flames, but also ablaze with the joyous anticipation of my punishment. A few are pious men and women who have come to see God's justice done. Most have come to witness the spectacle.

They have come to see me burn.

I strain against my binds, the pillar of wood at my back biting into my spine. But my weak struggle is of no use. My wrists, bound behind me, are raw and bleeding, and the rope at my neck only makes it harder to find air. I push hard against the pole and for a brief moment find the precious relief that I crave.

I focus my attention behind the mob, on the road to the

castle, and beyond to the endless blue sky. I hated the city when I came here as a child, and though I became accustomed to the constant stench and dark stone corners, I have never forgotten my early home in the Highlands. Once, I had the rich green earth to play upon and crisp country air to breathe. I let my eyes rest on the sky. That, at least, is the same. I try to soothe myself with this knowledge. I belong to Scotland.

My respite is short-lived. As I suck inky smoke into my lungs, they feel as though they are on fire, charred from within. Each breath is a fight. Still more horrible is the knowledge that the pain will only worsen. The flames lick at my bare feet with a sharp, piercing intensity as my skin begins to blister.

I look into the crowd, my watery eyes pleading, but I know I will find no aid from the masses gathered in the square. The congregated come from all walks of life, all classes, a few men dressed in full Highland kilt, others emulating the English with their breeches and jackets. Some are military men, garrisoned at the castle, looking for a story to tell their fellow soldiers when they return up the hill. The women mostly wear simple plaids, but one is in an elaborate dress, her lace bonnet framing her pretty face. An imposing man holds her close. An earl or a marquess, perhaps.

I try to focus on each individual, but my eyes snap back to the bishop, who stands in front, his torch held high in his hand, arm raised in righteous fury, face set in stone.

The blaze catches my skirts now and a searing pain travels up my leg. No matter how determined I am to remain distracted, there is no diversion in the world that can take my mind from the anguish. I have told myself that I willnae scream, willnae give them the satisfaction. But I cannae help the cry that escapes my lips, a sound as hideous as if it has come from the devil himself. I have become what they would believe me to be: inhuman.

I can no longer feel the agony in my feet and I am grateful for the rope around my neck. I cannae look down to see my blackened feet. It willnae be long now until the inferno engulfs me.

I look one last time to the crowd for any small comfort as my skin sizzles and my blood boils. All I see are faces filled with hatred. A child hides behind her mother, whose eyes blaze with a fevered glow to rival even the hellfire that swallows me in its gaping maw. I will find no sympathy here.

They have come to see the witch burn.

Another cry flies from my mouth but cuts short, ending in a sputter. I can no longer find the air to fill my lungs; there is only smoldering darkness. I try to embrace it, to put an end to the torture.

A few of the ladies gathered in front look ill now. They wanted to see me burn, but they weren't prepared for the cracking of my skin as it cooks on my bones, or the smell of charred flesh.

One girl pushes her way to the front of the crowd. The sight of her makes my heart soar. She will save me. I know she will. Hope floods my body, and I trick myself into believing that the flames have been extinguished. A new bout of pain pushes that thought from my head.

When I focus once again on the girl, my faith is dashed; my heart plummets back to the earth, shattering against the cold, unloving stone. I realize that she isnae here to save me. The last thing I see is her look of pure, triumphant joy. Hate fills my body as I, at last, pass into darkness.

2

heather

I CLOSE MY eyes and think of blood.

Count backward from ten, I tell myself. I grip the hard plastic of the chair and breathe in and out, slowly. It's a trick I learned in group, and sometimes it works. By the time I get to three the compulsion has passed, and I open my eyes with a sigh.

This is where I've spent the past six weeks of my life. Not quite a hospital room, not quite a prison cell; the walls are painted a tragic yellow-green. The room's contents come in pairs: two beds, one against each wall; two chairs; two desks. Each side a perfect mirror of the other. Except my side is neat and clean, while my roommate's looks like a tornado just passed through. I don't blame her. She's new

5

and hasn't had to face punishment for being messy. She will soon, though. Then she'll learn her lesson, just like I did. Also, my side looks bare because my things are all packed away. I glance at the duffel bag at my feet and rub my hands against my knees. I'm full of nervous energy.

Today I get to go home. I can't keep my feet still, and my heels bounce up and down on the worn gray linoleum. I wasted so much time here. Starting next month I get to spend the rest of my summer where I truly belong, where I get to spend every summer, where I should be right now: with my grandma and my aunt in Scotland.

I wait impatiently for Dr. Casella. She probably has to speak with my parents about my recovery process, remind them again that I need to take my meds every day. I feel like I'm being watched, and I glance up at the corners of the room, then close my eyes tight. There are no cameras. There is no one here. It's a side effect of the medication they have me on . . . this paranoia. The feeling is easy to ignore, much more so than my burning desire to leave this place, to be a thousand miles away on another continent. Much more so than the compulsion I've been forced to deny for six weeks.

The door flies open, and for a moment I think it's going to be Dr. Casella, but it's just my roommate, back from her group therapy session. She's framed by the doorway, and again I can't help but wince at how painfully thin she looks. She's one of those girls who thinks the less of her there is, the more she deserves love. There are a lot of them here at the Great Lakes Wellness Center. Girls with eating disorders. Not that I can judge. There are a lot of girls like me here too.

Though not exactly like me. In therapy they all had a story to tell about why they were the way they were, why they did what they did. I listened and nodded, and when it was my turn I talked about how hard my life was, how powerless I felt, because I knew it was what they wanted to hear. I'd do anything to get out of this place, to be labeled "better" and sent on my merry way.

"Leaving today?" My roommate is staring at me with her wide, round eyes. Her stringy dark hair frames her gaunt face. I nod.

"Lucky." She flops back on her bed, her bony arms and legs sprawled to the sides.

"You should straighten up your stuff," I tell her, feeling like I need to share my wisdom with the newbie. She just shrugs. "If you fail room inspection they'll make you scrub the communal toilets," I warn. That gets her attention and her head pops up.

"Hey, is what you told me yesterday true? Are they really watching us all the time?"

"I said that?" I know I did; my paranoia was particularly bad yesterday. Sometimes, despite my best efforts, I can't act normal. I crack a phony grin. "I was just messing with you."

"Oh, good." She sits up and lifts her shirt slightly. Around her skeletal middle she's taped a sandwich bag filled with a few ounces of water. "Every little bit helps," she tells me with a grin. Then walks to our private bathroom to, I assume, dump the evidence.

A lot of the anorexic girls try to trick the scales. It won't last long. Even if her pat-down didn't reveal her secret this time, she'll get caught eventually. It's harder for girls like me.

There's no use trying to trick anyone, not when they do a head-to-toe search daily. Dr. Casella promised that would stop when I left here . . . that I would once again be responsible for my own body. My roommate returns, sits on her bed, and pops her earbuds in.

"Heather, are you ready?" Dr. Casella asks from the doorway. I didn't even see her there. I grab my duffel and make a beeline for the door, but at the last moment I pause and turn back. "Good luck," I tell the flesh-and-bones stick figure of a girl. Then I follow Dr. Casella down the hall.

"Are you excited?" Dr. Casella asks me, her smile warm.

"To get the hell out of here?" I ask. "Only more excited than I've been for anything in like, my entire life."

Dr. Casella's laugh echoes as we pass through the door to the reception area, which her key card opens. My parents sit there with matching expressions of hope and fear. They want to know if their daughter is better. They want me to be returned fixed and whole, no longer broken.

I walk through the door with a fake smile plastered to my face. I'll do my best to convince them that the six weeks spent in this place has been a success. That I no longer think of blood.

Unfortunately, it's easier said than done.

3
heather
4 weeks later

"HEATHER!" I OPEN my eyes to see my dad's concerned face hovering over me. My bedroom is dimly illuminated by the light from the hall.

"Wh-what's going on?" I shiver against the cold, even though summer in Chicago is well under way and my mom hates to use the AC. I realize that my sheets are damp. My pajamas, too. I run a hand through my sweat-soaked hair.

"Are you okay?" My mom appears behind my father, worry etched in the lines around her eyes. I've been at home for a month now, but she treats me like I'm made of glass.

I sit up and cough uncontrollably. My throat is raw. I gulp down deep breaths until my coughing fit passes. "Was I screaming?" I ask hoarsely.

"Aye, and . . ." My dad glances at my mom.

She sits next to me on the bed. "Do you remember what you dreamt about?" she asks, smoothing back my hair. "It looked like you couldn't breathe."

"No." It's not quite a lie. The terror is already fading. There's no need to share my nightmare with her. Some things are better kept to the shadows.

My mom studies me, her eyes shining in the dull light. "The Wellness Center was supposed to help you."

"Dr. Casella said this could happen," I remind her. I don't want her to worry, but I'm shaken. Why did I dream of being burned alive as a group of onlookers gleefully watched? Why were all the people's clothes so old-fashioned? I know the location—it's near where my aunt lives in Scotland, on the road that leads up to Edinburgh Castle. Where I'm going today.

When my mom caught me cutting myself, it almost broke her. She's afraid something happened to me when I was younger. Something I'm too scared to tell her about.

The truth is, I don't know why I do it. Nothing traumatic happened the year it started—unless you count being one of the last girls in my class to get my period. I'm pretty sure if horrifying dreams were a side effect of that, I'd have learned about it in health class. I could pop a couple of Midols and call it a day.

"I want to get a little more sleep before my flight," I say, lying back down.

My father nods and makes his way toward my door while my mother just stares at me, her face stricken. For a moment panic fills me. If she tells me I can't go, I don't know what I'll do. I need to go.

"I'm okay, really," I tell her. She bends over and hugs me, pulling me to her. The damp fabric of my pajamas presses against my clammy skin. My hip aches, and when my mother stands I spot a bloom of fresh blood staining my pajama top. If she sees that, it's back to the Center for me. Back to pointless therapy, hospital food, and lights-out at eight-thirty.

Luckily my mother doesn't notice, and when she leaves, the door clicking behind her, I rush to my dresser and grab a handful of tissues. It will have to do until I can get a bandage, maybe at the airport, so my mother isn't suspicious. I decide to get dressed. It's only six in the morning, but there's no way I'll be going back to sleep.

I can hear them in the hall, whispering. My mother's high-pitched, anxious voice punctuates my father's much deeper cadence, his accent almost rhythmic. She wants me to stay here for the rest of the summer. She thinks I need more recovery time, more supervision, even though in the month since I've left the Wellness Center I've done everything they've asked, haven't missed a single therapy session.

I glance at my luggage, already packed and ready for my afternoon flight. "You know she loves Edinburgh," my father says, pronouncing Edinburgh as the Scots do, *Edinburra*. "It will be good for her. Not to mention Mum and Abbie need to see her."

"But what if she starts it up again?" My mother's pained voice cuts through our house.

Mom's the one who found me that day, my leg covered in blood. I thought I was home alone; I didn't bother to lock my door. All these years I've kept it a secret and in one moment my world came crashing down. I was supposed to leave for Scotland the next week, but instead I was sent off to the Wellness Center with other girls like me. Troubled, broken girls.

"I don't think the nightmare is a good sign. Maybe she's . . . she's . . ." She can't even say it out loud. That maybe it's all started again. If she comes to check my scars I'm screwed. I was home all of two hours before I found ten minutes alone with a sharp object. Even my mother can't watch me all the time.

"Maybe she just needs different medication," my father says. I shake my head. Even the drugs don't fight the compulsions.

I walk into the hall and their conversation halts. They stare at me, take in the fact that I'm no longer wearing pajamas but am fully dressed. "I'm hungry," I say with a forced smile. "Who wants pancakes?"

My father grins. "You're making them? Banana or chocolate chip?"

I raise my eyebrows. "Chocolate chip." I shake my head and give him a look that asks, *Is there any other kind?*

That finally gets a smile from my mom. She puts her arm around me as we walk down the stairs to the kitchen, giving me an extra squeeze before letting me go. I grab the flour and sugar and start gathering ingredients from the pantry.

"When I spoke with your aunt Abigail earlier," my mother says, sitting at the kitchen table, "she mentioned you made these for her last summer." She stops, then lets out a little sniffle. "She's looking forward to seeing you." She wipes away a tear and I feel a flood of guilt over the pain I've caused her.

"Did you tell her?" I ask quietly.

My mother glances at my father. "Of course we told her. She needs to know what's going on with you in case . . ." She pauses. "I'm really not sure you should go. Or maybe I should go with you. . . ."

My father puts his hand on her shoulder. "We've already discussed this, love." At Great Lakes I learned that one of the reasons for self-destructive behavior is not having enough control over your own life, feeling helpless. I brought this up with Dr. Casella and we had a whole session with my parents about it. Unfortunately, it seems to have made my mother even more protective.

She looks at him. "Our daughter just got out of a clinic for mentally unstable youth and you want us to send her halfway around the world?"

"It's been a month, Mom. And I'll be a phone call away."

She turns her gaze on me. "If you bother to answer. Last year I couldn't get ahold of you unless I used that texting apple thing. . . ."

"App, Mom," I say. It takes every ounce of willpower not to roll my eyes.

"I don't care what it's called," she snaps. "The point is that if I want to hear your voice, to make sure you're okay, I won't be able to. As if typing a message can take the place of a real conversation."

"Mom, I promise to always answer the phone when you

call, no matter what the time." I motion to myself, dressed and ready to go. "I'm better. I'll have my weekly sessions with Dr. Casella." I explain to her, again, that video chat will be just as good as seeing Dr. Casella in person. "I'll be fine."

I know that the best way to convince her is to just act like myself, to show her I'm no different than I was last year or the year before. That I'm still just me.

"Clearly you are not fine, Heather. Maybe the other thing is over, but you just had a violent nightmare." She sighs. "Maybe it's all the scary movies you guys watch."

"It's not the movies," my dad and I say at the same time, causing my mom to bark out an unexpected laugh. She's squeamish when it comes to horror films, but my dad and I both love the gore. Even when I was younger, I couldn't get enough. I knew it was just pretend, but I liked feeling scared and safe at the same time.

"Oh, that reminds me, I ordered *Blood Dawn* so you can download it," he says to me. We missed that one in the theater, thanks to my time at the Center.

"Thanks, Dad." I love creepy vampire films.

"And I have that list of things to bring back. I'll pay the fee for the extra luggage, so dinnae worry about that." After nearly twenty-five years in America, my father's accent has lessened, but it's not completely gone. *Do not* and *cannot* always come out like *dinnae* and *cannae*. "Just be sure to have your aunt take you shopping. . . . You're still too young to get the whisky I want."

My mother shoots him a look and my father shrugs.

"What? When you're Scottish, bottles of Scotch make

excellent presents for clients." My father is an architect. Forever ago he came to Chicago for school, met my mother, and decided to stay.

Since they're arguing about whether it's acceptable for their underage daughter to carry hard liquor across international borders, I know it's a done deal; my mom has been won over. They'll let me go visit the Scottish side of my family. I bang my hip against the counter and try to hide my wince of pain. I can't forget to get some bandages for the plane.

Maybe the night terror is related to the other thing . . . the thing I tried so hard to keep hidden from my parents, from everyone. The thing only recently forced into the light of day. The horrible dream and the strange need. I push the thought aside and cook breakfast for my parents, my throbbing hip bringing me comfort, making me forget the terror I felt in my dreams.

4

heather

AFTER SEVEN HOURS, three in-flight movies, and a crappy airline meal with a substance that may or may not have been chicken, I'm ready to crawl out of my skin. I get that feeling that someone is watching me. No one is, though. The other passengers are either sleeping or watching their miniscreens.

"I'm just being paranoid," I mumble, barely above a whisper.

But my blood is pounding in my ears. I wipe my clammy hands on my jeans. What if I started freaking out on the airplane? It would be beyond embarrassing, not to mention I'd most likely be banned from this airline in the future. I'd probably be on the news—my mother would never let me leave her sight again.

The thought makes my stomach hurt, and I feel suddenly ill. I grab my backpack from under the seat in front of me, push past the old woman beside me, and practically sprint down the aisle to the bathroom.

"Miss!" a flight attendant calls. "Miss, we're about to begin our descent. Please find your seat."

"It's an emergency," I say, squeezing myself into the bathroom and locking the door. I'm not usually claustrophobic, but I feel trapped. I heave my backpack onto the tiny counter next to the sink, wedging it in with my body so it doesn't fall over. With shaking hands I undo my pants so my hip is exposed. Quickly I pull off the bandage and throw it away.

I fumble with my backpack, trying to undo from the strap the attached pin that screams GO VIKINGS! in bright red letters. My school mascot. I rip the pin off, poking my pointer finger with the needle. A single drop of blood appears on my skin and the sight calms me. I suck on the pinprick and the salty, metallic taste steadies my nerves. Then I bring my attention to my hip.

Carved into the flesh is a small, neat pattern. I press the pin into the skin at the center of the coil and feel an instant release, my body going back to normal, the tension dissipating. I pull the pin out and tattoo the pattern, slowly and expertly.

I work smoothly, rhythmically. When I was thirteen, I used to scratch my skin just to see the blood, putting to use the X-Acto knife my parents bought me for school projects. Then I began to slash straight, neat lines on my upper thigh. After a while the incisions stopped giving me the much-needed feeling of release, and those scars have all but healed. Instead, I began to carve patterns in my skin. The three-tipped Celtic knot on my hip; an X on my inner thigh, a small circle in the middle; and on my upper arm just under my armpit, a spiral. I knew my parents would be horrified, but I see it as a kind of art. People get tattoos, don't they? How is this different?

I realized how very different it was when my mother walked in on me as I carefully sliced my skin. The look of horror on her face. I expected yelling, screaming, but her quiet revulsion was way worse. After five minutes on the computer, she phoned Great Lakes, and she and my dad shipped me off the next day. My dad was confused about the whole thing, hadn't seen what my mom had. The real me, knife in hand, covered in blood.

I think back to the time, years ago, when I would never have considered cutting myself. I hated the sight of blood—real blood, anyway. Now it seems so routine. Maybe I can be normal again. I glance at my reflection in the mirror, pin in hand, blood welling over the wound on my hip.

I am not normal.

A knock on the door interrupts my trance.

"Miss? You really must take your seat now."

"Just a minute!" I yell, replacing the bandage and doing my pants back up. I fasten the pin back on my bag—sharp objects may not be allowed on airplanes, but no one cares about a school spirit pin on a backpack—and give myself another look in the mirror. My hair is out of place from my nap, but other than that I look fine.

Calmed, I open the door. The stewardess glares at me, but I give her a smile and make my way back to my seat, the craving sated.

"Heeeea-ther!" My aunt waves at me as soon as I step out of the terminal.

I run to her, wrapping her in a big hug. She's the girl version of my father, tall and thin, with dark blond hair and deep blue eyes. I inherited the MacNair eyes, but my hair is a lighter blond, like my mother's.

"I missed you, love," my aunt says, giving me another hug. Her accent is heavier than my father's, since she's never left Scotland for anything longer than a few weeks of vacation every year. "I'm glad you're here." Each vowel is pronounced with great care, each *r* rolled to perfection.

"Me too, Aunt Abbie." Once we landed I felt a million times better, like I'm where I belong.

We grab my luggage and head toward her car. I automatically go to the right side before remembering the steering wheel is on the right in Scotland. "Are you driving?" my aunt teases.

"Not if we want to make it home alive," I say with a grin, walking around to the passenger side. "I've just gotten the hang of driving on the correct side of the road." That starts my aunt off on a rant about how the UK is right and the rest of the world got it wrong. It makes me smile to listen to her, getting used to her accent again. Usually by the end of the summer I have a slight Scottish twang myself, which amuses my father to no end. He calls me his "wee Scottish lassie" until it fades and I am once again his "American girl."

We drive past cottages and sheep until we get closer to the city, where the buildings are a strange blend of modern and Gothic. New structures stand alongside stone buildings hundreds of years old. Even the side streets feel old, cobblestone roads and small, dark alleyways. As we drive farther into the city center, the buildings become denser and there are all kinds of shops and restaurants.

"So Dad told you about . . ." I trail off lamely.

"Aye. They called me when you went into the . . . what do they call it?"

"Wellness Center. There were a lot of girls there with issues, like eating disorders and other stuff. One girl would pull out her hair, one strand at a time." I babble on, hoping to distract my aunt from talking about my issues, my problems.

"Well, your mum said that I'm to watch you like a hawk and make sure you're taking your medicine and staying healthy."

I nod. "It's not that I hate myself or anything like that," I try to explain.

"Love, if you're worried what I think, dinnae. Everybody has their secrets; everybody has their dark side. As long as you're getting better . . ."

"I am," I assure her quickly, and she flashes me a smile. I'm glad she doesn't think less of me. I want things to be the way they've always been between us.

Black cabs whiz by, zooming in and out of traffic. I ask

my aunt about the trip she's going to take to Australia. She's been planning it for years, and it's supposed to finally happen in the fall.

She doesn't seem to want to discuss it, though. When I press her, she says, "I'm no' sure I'll make it out there this year."

"I thought you were definitely going," I say, confused.

"Oh, nothing's set in stone."

I shake my head. "But, Aunt Abbie—"

"I meant to ask you about school." She cuts me off. I realize Aunt Abbie wants me to drop it, so I do. I'll ask her again later. Maybe she met someone, but that wouldn't prevent her from taking a two-week vacation.

"My mom's pissed that I've decided I want to go to film school," I say, changing the subject.

"Even when you were wee she talked about you becoming a lawyer. You know, she went to law school, but then . . . life happened."

"Meaning *I* happened," I say. "I don't know how to make her understand. . . ." I trail off as we turn onto Princes Street and I catch sight of Edinburgh Castle.

On one side of the street are department stores and shops; the other side is a well-manicured park, and above that an imposing stone structure built on an extinct volcano looms over the city. Rock juts out from the otherwise green hill. The castle itself is surrounded by a gray stone wall. I stare up at it as we drive by. I thought I'd feel better coming to Scotland, but the strange emptiness is still there. Was I wrong about needing to be here? Or is there someplace specific I should go. The castle? No, that doesn't feel right.

There's somewhere I need to be. The thought fills me with a strange dread, but also with a sweet anticipation. I shiver. This medicine is really messing with my head.

"She'll come around eventually," my aunt is saying. "What does your father say?"

I pull my eyes away from the castle. "Um . . . Dad? He's psyched. He thinks I'm going to be the next George A. Romero."

"Who?" she asks.

"*Night of the Living Dead*?" I prompt. Blank stare. "Never mind. How about Steven Spielberg?"

My aunt's face brightens. "Him, I've heard of."

It's taking us forever to go along Princes Street. Between the shopping and the park-goers, there are droves of people meandering around. We crawl along at a snail's pace, and my aunt curses.

"Move your arse! Cross at the crosswalk!" she yells. "You barmy idiot! I swear, I'm going to move to the country."

"You say that every summer," I remind her with a laugh.

"And every summer I mean it. Every dozy git that fancies themselves at all artistic flocks here for the festival and makes my life a living hell." Translation: My aunt is sick of all the hipsters who show up for the Fringe Festival every August. People from around the world come to Edinburgh and the city just vibrates with excitement.

Aunt Abbie glances at me. "I've taken a sabbatical this summer, so we have plenty of time to spend together." She's a librarian at the University of Edinburgh. I'm about to ask why she took the summer off instead of a vacation in the fall for her trip when she catches my questioning look and misinterprets its meaning. "I promise, I'm no' your jailor. I willnae take up all of your time. Fiona and Asha have already been asking after you . . . and Robert too."

I smile. I only get to see my "summer" friends a few months each year, but we've stayed close since I was little. I've been friends with them longer than with any of my friends back home. A little spike of panic rises up. "You didn't tell them about—"

"No, of course no'. That's for you to tell if you wish. Fiona got it into her head that you went to some film program, and that pretty much seems to be the consensus. Although she kept asking why you disappeared online."

I wasn't allowed to have my phone while I was at Great Lakes. Thinking of Fiona makes me think of all the other people I miss here. A blush rises to my face.

"And Alistair?" I ask, trying to make my voice casual, but I know I sound eager. My aunt flashes me a grin. I've been not-so-secretly in love with Robby's older brother, Alistair, forever. They're the sons of my aunt's friend, and we were always thrown together and told to go and play. Robby is my age, but Alistair is three years older. I had a crush on him before I even understood what having a crush meant.

"Alistair started university this year at St. Andrews. He's staying up there for the summer." She takes in my fallen face. "But Robert is around, giving ghost tours on the high street. You'll want to be seeing him."

I laugh. Robby is more annoying than anything else, always showing off and trying to get attention. "Of course I'll see Robby." I think of the last picture I saw of him, posted on his Instagram feed, making a goofy face. "But really I want to see Fiona and Asha. Can they come over soon?"

"Whenever you want. Friday I have dinner with a few colleagues from the university, just to catch up. You can have them over for the night. You'll have the place to yourself. There's plenty of room now that Mum is . . ." Her words hang heavy in the car.

"How is Gram?" I ask. My aunt lived with my grandma for years, which was fine when Gram was just a bit forgetful. This year her dementia got a lot worse and she had to be moved to an assisted living facility.

"Good. I think she's happy, though it's hard to tell."

"I can visit her, right?" I ask.

"As much as you'd like. But I have to warn you, Heather . . . she's no' all there." It takes me a moment to realize what my aunt has said. She drops the *t* when she says *not*, so my brain needs a moment to translate.

"She's worse than last year?" I ask, dreading the answer.

"Aye. I'm sorry, love. She's still your gram . . . just no' the way you remember."

I nod as we break free from Princes Street traffic and drive up the Mound, the hill that separates the "old" part of Edinburgh from the "new"; even the new part of the city is still pretty old. The street winds past the Scottish National Gallery and an assembly hall that looks more like a cathedral, to the Royal Mile, which leads to the castle. Once we cross the Royal Mile, also called the high street, it's only a few minutes to my aunt's flat. She lives right next to a large park called the Meadows.

As we're about to cross the Royal Mile, a man steps into the street, not even checking for traffic. My aunt honks her horn and curses again. "Bloody tourists!" she yells.

I smile. I may be an American, but I'm not a tourist. Not really. Scotland is in my blood.

5

ẖeaẖer

WE LUG MY bags up the stone steps to my aunt's flat. By the third landing Aunt Abbie completely breaks down into a coughing fit. She had part of her lung removed several years back and is usually fine but sometimes has trouble with physical activity. I help her up the stairs to the kitchen so she can rest and go back for my luggage. When I finally get it all inside, she seems to have recovered. She sits at the table, her breathing back to normal.

"Are you okay?"

"Aye, I was just having trouble catching my breath. I'm fine now."

"You just didn't want to help, right? There's nothing

wrong with you," I call out as I drag my bags across the living room to the tiny guest room where I always sleep. She gives me a strange look, then shakes her head.

"No, wait, Heather. Take Mum's room. It's bigger and looks out onto the park."

I haul my bag across the apartment to Gram's old room, turning the knob hesitantly. Strangely, when I push open the door I feel comforted. Most of her stuff is gone, but the room still smells like her. Her bed and dresser are here; even her sewing machine is still in the corner. I shove my luggage next to the bed. I can unpack later.

"Heather," my aunt calls from the kitchen. When I walk from my room she hands me a phone. "Same number as last year. Unlimited texts and data. It's been activated."

"Thanks, Aunt Abbie." I glance down at it and I already have a text from Fiona.

> *Heather! I'm so glad ur back. Work sux.*
> *Come save me!*

I smile. Fiona works at her mom's café with a not-so-secret smoldering resentment. I text her back:

> *Just arrived. I'll stop by this afternoon. Put*
> *aside some cake for me.* 😀

Her mother makes the best caramel sponge cake. Even Fiona has to admit that it's one of the perks of her family's owning the café.

No promises. Packed with Americans tourists
& they eat like pigs.

There's a few seconds' pause and then another text that reads:

No offense.

I sigh and shake my head. Fiona has no filter.

"Your parents will be wanting to know you've made it here safe and sound," my aunt reminds me. "They're probably waiting by the computer, since I said we could video chat as soon as we got home." She looks at the clock. "It's two a.m. in Chicago, so we should call them now so they can get to sleep. . . ." She pauses, hands flat on the counter, head hung forward. "Heather, there's something I have to tell you."

The floor drops out from under me. I know what she's going to say.

"It's back, isn't it?" My aunt has been in remission for almost five years. The lump on her lung was removed, and a course of chemo killed all the remaining cancer cells. Cancer-free is never a sure thing, though.

She nods slowly. "I just started chemo again, and . . . that's why Mum had to go into the home. It was just too much." She says it guiltily, like she should have done more.

"It's not your fault. . . . Wait. Is that why Dad came here in the spring?" He'd said it was to help move Gram.

"I wanted to tell you face to face, love. And then you

were getting help yourself. I had to beg your mother to send you along after. I wanted us to have the summer together, just in case."

My anger diffuses, leaving behind a layer of frustration. My aunt just told me she could die. It's weird when people talk like that about their own deaths. It all makes sense now: Mom's teary eyes when she mentioned Aunt Abbie. My parents letting me come to Scotland, even though they were clearly concerned. My aunt's sabbatical, her canceled travel plans. Her coughing fit.

"Okay, let's call Mom and Dad . . . and then I'm making you a special batch of chocolate chip pancakes . . . if you're up for it."

My aunt nods and gives me a sad smile. "Sounds perfect."

I study my aunt. Last time she had chemo she didn't lose her hair, though she said the nausea was unbearable. She does look thin now, worn. I'll have to make sure she takes care of herself.

She puts her arm around me and walks me to the den. As we talk to my parents I try to put on a brave face, but all the while my hand is at my hip. I picture the three-curved symbol, cutting into it with a nice sharp knife, the blood welling and slowly dripping down my leg. The image soothes me. Sometimes thinking about cutting allows me to put off the actual act, while still feeling that sense of relief that it brings. I don't let myself think about how abnormal that is, not now, not when I've wondered a thousand times what is wrong with me.

Instead, I focus on the blood, and it calms me.

In the afternoon Aunt Abbie wants to take a nap. Despite her enthusiasm for my pancakes, she only picked at her break-fast, barely eating. She looked ill, like if she ate any more than a bite she would puke. It scares me to see her like this. Last time she was sick I was too young to understand. That's when my parents spent their summers in Edinburgh as well, before my mom started working again and my dad became so in-demand in Chicago. I remember they were worried, but my aunt seemed strong and always had a smile on her face. I knew she would be okay.

But that was before I was overtaken by the strange com-pulsion to cut my skin, to watch my blood spill. My world has changed since then, and I'm no longer an optimistic eleven-year-old.

I tell my aunt that if she wants to take a nap I'll nap too, although that's the worst thing I can do for jet lag.

She gives me a look. "Heather, go see your friends. Have fun. Explore the city. Enjoy the festival. There are a million things you could be doing, and hanging around here while I take a nap should not be one of them."

"You don't want to . . . I don't know, supervise me?"

She sighs. "I promised your mum, but as long as neither of us tells her . . . no harm done." She gives me a playful shove. "Now go!"

"Okay, I know when I'm not wanted," I tease. I grab my phone, some cash that my aunt left for me, and my hoodie, because even though it's clear and sunny now, in ten minutes it could be raining. Just some of the charm of Scottish weather.

I also grab my camera bag and sling it across my shoulder. It's my travel camera, nothing like the super-expensive one I have at home, but I still love it. It's small and shoots great video. Maybe I can get some "mood" shots of Edinburgh.

It's a nice day, warm and bright. Instead of heading across the park to Fiona's family's café, I take a detour through a few of the University of Edinburgh buildings. The yearly festival uses almost every available meeting space, and there's a ton of stuff to see. People stand outside performance spaces and hand out flyers. Within minutes I have one for a comedy troupe performing improv, a book signing for a romance author, and a rap performance of *Romeo & Juliet*. I feel guilty dumping them in the garbage, so I tuck the papers in my back pocket.

There's an art installation that has giant teddy bears posed in an office room. One is stationed at a computer, while another sits at a desk with a cup of coffee. Not sure what it's meant to represent, but it looks interesting.

I film the installation and do a sweep of the crowd. There are carnival rides set up off to the side. A lot of people are just enjoying the day, playing Frisbee and picnicking.

As I step onto the grass, anxiety overtakes me, an all-too-familiar feeling. I look around, expecting to spot at least one person staring at me, but I'm just another girl in the crowd.

"I'm just being paranoid," I chant. "This isn't real."

My mantra doesn't work, and I feel the overwhelming urge to cut. Sometimes I can fight it. I did for six whole soul-crushing weeks. I count backward from ten. At two, the impulse passes, but it leaves me shaky and drained.

I must be more jet-lagged than I realize. The sun glaring off the grass is hurting my eyes.

The grass is so vibrant, it's surreal.

I hear laughter, the sounds of children playing echoing in my ears.

6

primrose

August 1, 1621
The Highlands

I RUN ALONG the hill, my bare feet wet from the dewy tufts of grass. Playing Ghost in the Graveyard gives me the chance to run like a deer, a habit of mine of which Da doesnae approve. Girls shouldnae run around like wild savages, he would say. Girls should stroll along at a gentle pace. Like the babbling brook near our home. Mam says I'm more like a mighty river after it has rained: loud, wild, and hard to control.

I still dinnae see my quarry, and I am about to give up and move on to another hiding place when I spot her down by the brook, hiding in the brush. She wears the same shapeless shift that I do, the white stark against the brown-green of the earth. I shriek in triumph and she turns on her heels to run; the coarse material of her dress billows in the wind. It gives her an unearthly look, as if she really is a ghost.

I sprint after her, quickly gaining ground, and I ken she can feel me behind her. She hazards a glance over her shoulder, but it's too late. My hand is already outstretched; my fingers graze her sleeve. I grin and shout, "You are caught, ghostie!" and she stops suddenly, causing me to crash into her. We both fall to the soft earth, laughing.

"It isnae fair," she says, pouting between giggles. I've always been able to beat Prudence at a footrace. Playing Ghost in the Graveyard is just as easy. I always find her, and when she tries to run, I always catch her. Sometimes, when I'm the ghost, I run very slowly just to let her win. It's no fun to always lose.

"I dinnae ken why I am faster," I admit.

"Da said we shouldnae say ken," she tells me with a superior look. Da likes us to sound English, as they do in Edinburgh. We arenae allowed to speak Gaelic at all.

"I dinnae know why I'm faster," I say. "Maybe because I'm older."

"By just a few breaths."

"A few breaths can make all the difference." I stand and help her up. We're exactly the same height, tall for our ten years. We share everything, even a face. No' even Da can tell us apart, although Mam never seems to have trouble knowing which one of us she's talking to. It's irritating when I'm trying to get out of a scolding.

Mam calls out from the cottage for us to go inside. I glance at Prudence. It is time for our secret learning, the kind only Mam can teach us. The things we learn from her we have to keep secret from everyone . . . even Da. Especially Da. He's unhappy enough that Mam knows how to read and taught us. He thinks the more women learn, the more likely we are to be tempted to evil things. He says girls' minds are simple, and can only handle simple things. But Mam says what men think they ken but dinnae can fill all the lochs in Scotland.

Prudence hooks her arm through mine and we make our way back to the cottage. Its stone walls and thatched roof are welcoming, as is the hearth that keeps our one-room house warm and cozy. I wish we could live here always, Mam and Prudence and me. I wouldnae even mind if Da stayed away in Edinburgh longer. He is always taking trips there, visiting family, selling our wool. He wants to take Prudence and me with him sometimes, but Mam says that Edinburgh is no place for us. That the city is filthy and the air foul. Usually Da has the final say, but on this one thing, Mam got her way. Prudence said Mam withheld her womanly charms . . . which means she slept in the bed with us for a few nights and Da got lonely without her.

Prudence and I walk over the threshold together and Mam looks up from the table. It is brimming with plants and flowers, beautiful and fragrant. Before her is a big book, her grimoire. It holds all her secrets. Da is to never see it, never to ken about it.

Mam smiles her broad, kind grin. "Sit, lassies. Your da is expected back tonight, so this is our last lesson for a while."

Prudence and I nod and go to the table, settling in on

either side of Mam. I stare at the grimoire, so close all I have to do is reach out to touch its pages. But I stop myself. That book is full of magic. No' the magic of fairy tales, which are just made-up stories, but real magic. Magic that uses the power of herbs and flowers and nature. Magic that heals.

7
ḥeatḥer

I STRAIGHTEN UP, my eyes darting around the Meadows, but the park is normal. Everything is normal. A few people are looking at me. "All right, love?" a man calls to me. "Looks like you've seen a ghost." I wave him off and take a deep breath, stumbling on the path through the park. After a few steps I start to feel better, and let out a small, shaky laugh. The man said I looked like I've seen a ghost, and it gives me an idea.

I phone Fiona. "On your way?" she asks without saying hello.

"Yeah . . . you know your mom's wedding dress from when she married Doug?"

"That hippie thing that looks like an old nightgown? How could I forget?"

"Would she let you borrow it?"

"Is this a film thing?"

"Maybe," I tell her.

"Can we not just have a coffee?" she asks with an exaggerated sigh.

"That's boring . . . but I guess I can just come by the café. . . ."

"Absolutely not. I want to get out of here. Let's meet at the Starbucks on the high street."

"Starbucks? Your mom is going to have a fit."

"I know. I can't wait for the look on her face when I tell her. See you there in twenty?"

"Okay. And don't forget the dress," I say before she hangs up.

I buy some baby powder and super-pale makeup at a pharmacy, pushing past the throngs of tourists meandering up the Royal Mile. When I finally make it to Starbucks, Fiona is waiting for me.

"Fiona!" I call, and wave to her. She's tall and slim, with a mop of curly reddish-orange hair. Her long legs poke out from under the table, making sure no one steals the extra chair. Slung over her own chair is a big canvas bag, the white material of the dress spilling out of it.

When I reach her she stands and pulls me in for a hug and then nearly falls on top of me when someone elbows past her. "I feel like we're going to be trampled at any moment," I say.

"Welcome to Edinburgh during the festival. I know one of the baristas, so I jumped the line," she tells me, sitting and pushing a cup toward me. "Vanilla latte, extra sugar, right?"

"You remembered." I let out an exaggerated sniffle. "I'm touched."

She sips her own giant iced coffee. "I've missed you, Heather. Most of my mates have left for the summer."

"Oh yeah, I saw Deirdre and Lexi's pics from Spain." Deirdre and Lexi are Fiona's school friends.

"Yeah, they're living it up in Ibiza while I'm stuck here."

"Well, if you were in Ibiza, you wouldn't be here with me," I point out.

She raises her eyebrows. "I love you, Heather, but have you seen the boys there? Mmmmm."

"I don't know, Scottish boys are pretty cute," I say. My face reddens and I chug my coffee.

"You mean Alistair is pretty cute," she says. I shrug, my face burning.

"So, what did you want this dress for?" she asks, motioning to the bag.

"Well, I have an idea for a short film. Are you in?" Fiona is my go-to actress.

"Of course I'm in. . . . Wait, am I going to have to learn to juggle?"

I laugh. Last year I was going to make a scary movie about killer clowns, but everything turned out to be so ridiculous, it was a hilarious disaster. "No juggling, I promise."

I pull out the baby powder and makeup and wave it around. "How would you like to be a ghost?"

After we leave Starbucks, we wait in line on the hard stone ground that leads to the castle. Fiona glares at the people behind us who are standing really close. Like those extra six inches are going to save them so much time. "Oi, ever hear of personal space?" She turns back to me. "Bloody tourists."

When we get inside instead of going straight up to where all the historical stuff is, we cut left and head down the stairs to the bathrooms. Fiona slips the dress over her clothes and I do her hair; scrunching it up so it looks even more wild than usual. I pour the powder on while she plasters the foundation on her face.

She studies herself in the mirror. "I look like I'm mental."

"It's going to read great on camera," I assure her.

I grab the bag and walk with her up the stairs and out onto the battery that leads to the part of the castle that's now the war museum. There's an overhang that looks over all of Edinburgh. I evaluate the shot area, gray stone castle walls on one side, scenic Scotland on the other.

"Perfect," I say.

"Are you supposed to be up there?" a castle employee in a blue vest calls out to us. He's clutching a walkie-talkie.

Fiona turns her gaze on him. "No, I'm bloody well dressed like this for my health. If you dinnae mind, we're trying to film here."

"All right, all right, no need to jump down my throat," he mutters, and walks away.

I give Fiona a look and she shrugs. "Most people don't want to deal with you if you act like you're a terribly important bitch." Then she grins. "Heather, do you remember when we were twelve and Robby called you a bitch for not letting him borrow your video game thingy?"

"Yeah." I shake my head. "I punched him in his face and was grounded for two weeks."

"He had to get his nose reset."

"And I had to make a show of apologizing." I shake my head. "I was going to tell him that if he ever called me that again, I'd break his nose again. But when I spoke with him, *he* apologized to *me*."

"I didn't know that part of the story," Fiona says.

"Yeah, good times when we were twelve." I laugh. "Okay, let's get some shots. I'm thinking of a whole 'Haunted Edinburgh' series. Why don't you start along the wall, in the shadows, and then step out into the light. I'll do a washed-out effect." I pause. "Fiona?"

"Yeah?"

"Ghosts don't wear sneakers."

"These trainers are new." I just stare at her pointedly. "Bloody hell, Heather," she says, giving in. "I'd better not get foot rot from this." She slips off her shoes and socks and tosses them to me. I tuck them in her canvas bag and get into position against the outer wall.

Fiona walks forward, doing a great job of looking ethereal until she reaches me. She sticks out her tongue and makes a razzing noise.

"Very professional. Let's do it again." I hoist myself onto the wall.

"Okay, that is definitely not safe," she says.

"It's going to look great from this angle. Let's go again."

Fiona seems to float along the stone as the wind pulls at her dress and hair. I won't even have to do too much editing to make her look ghostly.

"Got it," I tell her. I look around. "Let me get some shots of the city."

"Maybe we should do a murder scene," Fiona is saying. "Robby could be my lover who murders me in a fit of jealousy."

"Uh-huh." I pan the camera across the horizon, then look down. It's a long fall. I scoot forward. There's a sound in the distance that I can't quite make out. It tickles my mind, like I should know what it means, if I can just get closer. I lean forward, leaning, leaning . . .

"Heather!" Fiona shouts, and I'm pulled backward, my camera spiraling from my hands. I fall the five feet to the hard stone ground.

"Ow. What the hell?" I'm flat on my back, staring into the clear blue sky.

Fiona's face appears above me. "You looked like you were about to fall."

"I was just getting a shot." I pull myself up. "I dropped my camera," I say, panicking. "We have to go get it." There are paths that crisscross on the land beneath the castle, through parks and homes and cemeteries.

"Even if we could find it, it's smashed into a gazillion pieces," she tells me, peering down.

I let out a frustrated gasp. "There goes my summer film

project." At least it was my cheap camera. Still, I didn't want to lose it.

"Well, while we've been up here, random tourists have been snapping photos of me," Fiona says. "Let's set up on the esplanade with the castle in the background and charge a pound a shot. You'll be able to afford a new camera in no time."

"Fiona, you're brilliant," I tell her, feeling kind of shaky from my near fall. What was I thinking?

Fiona's a big hit, but I don't make nearly enough money for a new camera. Instead, Fiona and I blow it on shopping on Princes Street.

When I get back to my aunt's flat, without Fiona or shopping to distract me, I can't stop thinking about what happened back at the castle. I was just trying to hear that sound, but for a brief moment I forgot about everything—including my own safety. I swallow. It's over now, and I'm safe. But it's already consumed me, the awful need. There's no ignoring it this time, no pushing down the compulsion. There's only one way to stop these horrible feelings.

I go straight to my room and start tugging open the drawers to the sewing desk, searching until I find a pair of small silver scissors. They're sharp to the touch. They're perfect.

I pull up my sleeve, and looking in the mirror, I begin to carve, slowly and painstakingly tracing the spiral pattern. Immediately I feel better.

"Heather! Are you back?" my aunt yells from the hallway, causing me to jerk my hand and slash my skin, marring the mark. Blood pours down my arm, staining my shirt. I stare at the ruined symbol for a moment, anxiety flooding my body and making me tremble. I wrecked it.

"Heather!" Aunt Abbie calls again.

I tug off my shirt and ball it against my arm, looking for the bandages I bought at the airport in Chicago. Quickly I slap one on the cut and put on a fresh shirt.

"Here!" I call, throwing open the door. My aunt stands in the hall looking tired, her hair disheveled. "How was your nap?" I ask, trying not to sound as panicky as I feel.

"Fitful . . . I'm finding it hard to sleep lately." When she turns away from me I rub my sore arm, willing myself to calm down.

"I just went for a walk." I tell her about the art installation, babbling on.

She laughs. "Social commentary with teddy bears."

The sound of her laughter grounds me, makes me feel more like myself. "*Giant* teddy bears," I correct her.

"That I'll have to see."

If only my camera weren't smashed into a million pieces. Well, she doesn't have to know about that. "And I have these." I pull out the flyers I shoved into my pocket. "If you want to check out a show later."

"Oh, this could be fun . . . improv comedy. Should we go?"

"Sure," I answer quickly, though my aunt looks as if she doesn't have enough energy to make it down the stairs. "Sounds good."

"Okay, love. Let me see if I can rally. I'm going to put the kettle on. Want a cup of tea?" My aunt and my dad share the belief that a cup of tea solves any problem. Gram taught them that. "Robby's mom sent it over. . . . It's one of her herbal concoctions."

"Sounds great. I'll be right there." I turn to go back into my room to clean up a bit. No sooner have I closed the door than I hear a crash.

Aunt Abbie is sprawled on the kitchen floor in a pool of murky brown water, still clutching the kettle. "Aunt Abbie!" She doesn't respond. I grab my phone and dial 911, but then I remember that won't work here. I hang up and phone 999. They promise to send an ambulance right over.

The bandage from my arm has come undone and blood drips on the floor, mixing with the spilled water.

"Please be okay," I whisper next to my aunt's ear as I kneel beside her. "Please don't die."

8

heather

BY THE TIME the ambulance arrives my aunt is awake and talking. She tries to get up but I tell her she should wait.

She gives me one of her I-don't-know-what-the-big-deal-is looks. "I feel fine, Heather. Honestly."

"You *fell*. You were passed out for like, five minutes." I'm not going to let her brush this off. "You're *not* okay."

She allows the paramedics to check her out and she tells them about the cancer and the chemo and promises to go see her doctor right away. She says she skipped lunch and it was probably a blood sugar thing.

They seem satisfied and leave, but still, I'm not happy

and I insist she call her doctor and make an appointment for the next day.

After she hangs up, she looks at me, head tilted. "You know," she says, surprise in her voice, "I really am a wee bit hungry. Would you mind terribly making pancakes again, or are you sick of them?"

"No . . . I mean yes. I'll make them. Are you sure you're feeling okay?" I'm completely exhausted. Worrying about Aunt Abbie is draining. I don't want to show her how tired I am, not when she's so sick herself.

"I feel great," she tells me with a grin.

I make another batch of pancakes. I don't care if she only picks at them. I'd make her a million pancakes if it would make her happy. To my shock, she digs into the stack, devouring bite after bite.

"Um . . . whipped cream?" I ask.

"Aye, please," she says with her mouth full. "This is just . . . beautiful," she adds, savoring each morsel.

After she polishes off the plate she sits back with a satisfied grin, her hand rubbing her stomach. "I havenae enjoyed a meal like that since I started this round of chemo. I feel really good."

"I'm glad," I say as I clean up. "Since they're like, the only thing I know how to make." I glance at her. "But if you feel so good . . . why did you faint?"

"I dinnae know." Again, the it's-not-a-big-deal look, as if passing out is something normal people do on a regular basis. "I'll go to the doctor tomorrow and we'll see what he says. Dinnae worry, Heather."

"Don't worry?" I slam the pan down in the sink. I turn to her. "I found you unconscious on the kitchen floor!" I take a breath and say a little more calmly, "I thought you were going to die."

She grimaces. "I'm sorry I scared you . . . it isnae like I was having a go at you. It wasnae a prank." She smiles and I can't help but smile back.

"I know."

"And I'm fine now. More than fine. I think we should go to the comedy show and then grab dinner after. How's that sound?"

"That would be . . . great," I tell her, turning back to the dishes. I'm glad she says she's feeling better, but I'm scared she's just putting on a good face for me. I'm not a small child anymore, clueless to her pain. I make a promise that I will help my aunt as much as possible while I'm here.

Abbie and I spend the next morning at the hospital, where she has a full examination, complete with a blood draw and an X-ray. Afterward I head to Asha's house, my head full of worry and fears. I had another strange dream last night. I can't quite remember what it was about. I just know that I woke with a sore throat and a pounding heart.

I'm almost there when I get a text from Fiona, bringing me back from the dark shadows of my dreams to the bright sunshine of the day.

My parents are driving me mental!

I smile. I love Fiona.

> *Getting to Asha's now, can you hang out with us?*

> *No, I have to work. What about later?*

> *Okay, call me.*

I think that's the end of it, but within seconds Fiona texts:

> *My mum told me your aunt was sick again. Is she okay?*

> *Yes, they just need to run a few tests.*

> *What kind of tests?*

Then, immediately after,

> *Is it serious?*

I'm standing in Asha's doorway when she pokes her head out the door. "Heather!" She squeals and tackles me. It kind of takes me by surprise. While Fiona is wild and crazy, Asha has always been more reserved.

I grin. "Hi!" My phone dings and Asha takes a step back and smiles.

"Let me guess . . . Fiona?" she asks. I notice she's started wearing eyeliner and mascara, accentuating her dark eyes. And while she's always been thin, now she's curvy too.

"The one and only. Who else text stalks like she does?"

Asha grabs my hand and drags me inside. I love the way her house smells, like turmeric and cinnamon. The décor is interesting too, a mix of East and West. Kind of like her family. Her grandparents moved here from India, and both of her parents were born here.

I wave to her mom, who sits at the kitchen table sipping tea. She's wearing yoga pants and a T-shirt. Next to her sits Asha's grandma, in a traditional sari.

"Hello, Mrs. Khatri." I turn to Asha's grandmother. "Hi, Awa Khatri." Awa is what Asha calls her grandma.

Mrs. Khatri grins at me. "Hello, Heather. It's so nice to see you again."

Asha's grandma nods. "Good girls. Good, good girls."

"Thanks, Awa," Asha tells her fondly. "Mum, we're just going to my room for a bit."

"All right. Don't forget you have to meet your father at the library at four." Asha's dad works with Aunt Abbie at the university. He's a librarian for the history department.

"Oh, wait," I say before Asha drags me away. "I'm having a sleepover tomorrow night. Can Asha come?"

"Yes, of course." Mrs. Khatri pauses. "Is it okay with Abbie?"

"Oh, yeah. She insisted." I wave my hand and do my best Aunt Abbie impression. "'The world doesnae stop because Abigail MacNair has cancer. Invite your friends over. I'm still going to dinner with *my* friends.'"

I expect them to laugh, but all I get is silence. "So, she's fine with it," I say lamely. Asha's grandma stands and comes over to me, wrapping me in a big hug.

"Awa!" Asha says, but I don't mind.

I follow Asha to her room, collapse on her bed and quickly text Fiona.

Sleepover at my place tomorrow? 7pm.

Fiona responds immediately.

I'm there. Tell Abbie we love her!

Asha sits next to me on the bed. "So, how is your aunt really?"

I sigh. "She fell yesterday, but then she bounced right back. We went to a comedy show, and after that we found an Italian restaurant. She ate a huge plate of fettuccine Alfredo without vomiting afterward. In the world of chemo that's pretty impressive."

"So it's looking good?"

"Definitely." I don't tell Asha that the doctor explained that the chemo wasn't working as well as they'd hoped and they can't operate because of the placement of the tumor. I hear the doctor's words echo in my head. *Unfortunately, Ms. MacNair, it seems that your body is resisting the chemo. Your cells are dividing normally without being destroyed and unfortunately, that means the tumor has continued to grow.* I was so stressed when I heard all this that I rubbed my nail raw, causing it to bleed.

"Has she lost her hair?" Asha asks, pulling at her own long black braid.

"No. She didn't last time either." I take a deep breath. "She's doing fine. Let's talk about you, though . . . and your boyfriend." I grin. "I haven't been online lately, and when I go on all I see are pictures of you and some guy. I'm surprised he's not here now!"

"Well, we've only been together for a month. When I turned sixteen my parents decided I could date." Asha's parents have always been really strict.

"So who is he?"

She gives me a funny look. "You don't know?"

I shake my head.

"Remember Robby's friend Duncan?"

"Duncan? Long-haired metal-band freak Duncan?" I ask.

Asha's face pinches. "He's gotten a haircut since you last saw him."

"Yeah, no kidding. I didn't recognize him at all. When did you decide you liked him?"

"It just sort of happened. Fiona and I went over to Robby's and Duncan was there. He'd just cut his hair and I realized how cute he was and we started talking about . . . I don't even remember what. Then he asked me out."

I send Robby a text.

Back in town. Meeting up with Fiona & Asha
for a sleepover tomorrow. Want to hang with
the girls?

I look up and catch Asha raise her eyebrows. "What?" I ask. "It's rude to read over people's shoulders, you know," I joke.

"Are you sure it's okay to invite Robby? Your aunt won't mind a boy being there when she's out?"

"A boy?" I say, trying to understand. "You think my aunt would be worried that something would happen with me and Robby?" I laugh but she purses her lips. "I've known him since I was a baby."

My phone buzzes.

As much as I hate to miss a good pillow fight, I'm working tomorrow night.

Oh yeah, heard about the new job. Sounds cheesy.

Meet up Saturday? I'll get you on the after-noon tour for free. *. 3 p.m. Princes Street Gardens by the Scott Monument.*

Ha ha. I'll be there.

Asha and I talk about the internship she's doing at the library with her father and all the books she's been reading. Her parents push her, but not in a crazy-tiger-mom kind of way. More in a we-want-you-to-have-advantages-in-life kind of way. I'm sort of jealous of how normal she is.

My aunt picks me up at four, and she seems better than

she did yesterday, but I must be giving her pretty pathetic looks because she finally says, "Heather, it seems bad, but I'm no' giving up. I feel fantastic. I'm no' done with life just yet."

I sigh. "Then why did you cancel your travel plans? You've been talking about taking a trip to Australia forever, and now you're just fine with not going?"

"It's more complicated than that," she says. "Please, try to understand. I just want to focus on getting better now."

I nod and keep quiet on the drive home. I wonder if this is the last summer I will spend with my aunt. I haven't even seen Gram yet.

"Can we stop by the nursing home?" I ask. "I just want to make sure Gram's okay."

My aunt doesn't answer and I wonder if she heard me. I'm about to ask again when she says, "I check in with her nurses every day. Today they said she's no' doing well. It would be best to wait until she has a good day."

"What does a bad day mean?"

"It means that if we go today, she won't know who you are."

"I still want to see her," I insist.

On the outside the home looks like a small hospital, which, I suppose, it is. My aunt signs in and talks with the receptionist for a moment. She waves hello to one of the nurses and stops to speak with an elderly woman who asks after my dad. She must have met him in the spring. I wonder what's wrong with the woman, or if she's just too old to take care of herself.

We make our way through a common area and down a hall. My aunt stops at a door.

"This is it," she tells me, pushing it open. Gram's room is nicer than I expected. It looks comfy, like her old room in my aunt's flat. There are pictures of her family and friends everywhere, knickknacks she's collected over the years, and an obnoxious number of doilies. It screams "An old British lady lives here!" It's perfectly Gram.

She sits on her bed, staring at the wall. "Gram," I say, and she turns toward me. Her gray-white hair is cropped short and she wears a simple blue housedress. Her face is blank.

"It's me . . . Heather."

"Heather?" she repeats softly. Her eyes focus on me. "Are you a friend of Abigail's?"

"No . . . I . . ." I don't know what to say.

"Well, if you must see her, be quick about it. Michael is taking the entire family on holiday, to Italy, if you can believe it." Michael is my grandfather who died before I was even born.

"I remember that holiday," my aunt says, appearing at my side. "I was twelve and we spent a week in Florence. Your father was ill the entire time . . . stomach flu. He didnae even leave the hotel. He was so mad that I came home with a tan and he didnae. No' that he *can* tan."

"No, he just burns," I say quietly. I see that my grandma is losing focus. "Have a lovely time on your trip."

"Thank you, dear. So polite . . . Abigail should invite you around more often," she murmurs absently, turning away.

"I know you wanted to see her, Heather," my aunt tells me as we're walking back to the car. "But when she's like this you can't get through to her. She gets stuck in a time in her life and you have to wait for her to find her way back. She has better days, though." She puts her arm around me. "She'll even know who you are sometimes.

"Look, it's no' hard to get here. You can just hop on the bus, I'll show you which one. Come back and visit her anytime. We'll call first and see what kind of a day she's having."

I nod and get into the car. Seeing Gram like that was horrible, and I can feel the need building up inside me. I try to ignore the urge that drives me to cut myself, but I know that when I get home, I will bleed.

My aunt leaves me to my thoughts as we drive the rest of the way home, leaves me to the silent tears that flow down my face. She understands that sometimes you just have to cry.

9

heather

"HEATHER!" FIONA BURSTS through the doors, a hurricane of red hair and vanilla body wash. "I brought snacks and some films and gossip about . . . Where's Abbie?"

"Out with friends."

"The librarians are having a pish-up," Asha says from the doorway. With Fiona's grand entrance I hadn't even noticed her there. "My dad too." Her long black hair is pulled into a high ponytail.

"Translation," Fiona says loudly. "They're out to get drunk."

I roll my eyes. They act as if I'm a complete foreigner.

"Okay," I say, leading them into the living room. "First things first. Gossip." Before my aunt left she told me she knew it was hard, but I should enjoy myself. She didn't want me sitting around worrying about her or Gram, since there was nothing either of us could do about it.

"You mean about Asha's sex life?" Fiona screeches as she tumbles onto the couch, stretching her long legs out and putting her hands behind her head. "Maybe she'll give you the details, because she doesnae tell me."

Asha throws a pillow at her and sits next to me on the floor. I smile, remembering Robby's pillow fight comment. "That's personal," she tells Fiona with a huff. Asha has more of a posh, "proper" Scottish accent than Fiona.

"You don't have to tell us if you don't want to," I say. "How is it going with you two? How did you convince your parents it was time to let you date?" I ask Asha.

"I promised it wouldn't interfere with my studies or my internship. I asked them to trust me, and they do."

"That would never work on my parents," I say. Not that I've given them much reason to trust me.

"Yeah, so all those sham group outings ended," Fiona chimes in. "Asha and Duncan were always coupling off anyway, and I was stuck with Robby."

"Like you minded that," Asha shoots back. "You're the one always going on about how cute he is."

"Whoa," I cut in. "Hold up. Robby. Our Robby. Dorky, short, chubby Robby?"

Asha and Fiona exchange a glance. "Heather, you haven't seen him in what, a year? He's grown up quite a bit."

"Okay, I've seen him on Instagram."

"Those goofy pics?" Asha laughs. "He just does those for a laugh. He's actually quite cute."

"He's really, really fit," Fiona confirms. "Not that I'm sweet on him or anything, but a girl can look, cannae she?"

"More like drool," Asha jokes, and this time she's the one who gets smacked in the face with a pillow.

"Are you guys teasing me? The old 'let's make fun of Heather because she's American' bit?" I ask.

"No, he really is hot now," Fiona tells me. I look to Asha. She shrugs. "He's changed. I think he's actually been changing for a few years now, but you're so hung up on Alistair, you never took a proper look at Robby."

"I am not hung up on Alistair," I protest. "I just think he's a good person."

"Oh, Alistair," Fiona says in a mocking falsetto. "You're such a good person. And you're so big and strong. Can I help you toss your caber?"

My face warms. I try to change the subject from my longtime unrequited crush. "Well, I'll get to witness Robby's miraculous transformation for myself soon. I'm seeing him tomorrow afternoon at his ghost tour thingy."

"Woooo, Robby in a kilt," Fiona sighs. "I believe our Heather is in for a treat."

I laugh. "I don't know what spell you two are under, but I've known Robby . . . forever. I'm sure I'm immune to his charms."

"We'll see." Asha shrugs. "Hey, whatever happened with you and Derrick?"

"Derrick?" He was a guy I hung out with last year, but there was no chemistry. We both liked movies, but he was into pretentious foreign films and acting like he knew everything. "We broke up. We weren't really compatible."

"Meaning . . . the sex wasn't good?" Fiona asks with a mischievous smirk.

"Okaaaaay." I clap my hands together and ignore her. There's no need to discuss my utter lack of any experience when it comes to boys. "I need some candy."

"Sweets for everyone!" Fiona yells, throwing the candy up in the air. Asha rolls her eyes, then lets out a laugh. "I don't know how you can eat all that processed rubbish."

"Well," Fiona says, taking a mouthful of chocolate, "when your mom pretty much lets you do whatever you want *and* owns an organic foods café, the only way to rebel is to eat this *processed rubbish*."

Asha shrugs. "I'm training for a 10K. Either of you want to run with me tomorrow, just up to Hollyrood Park and the Crags?"

Hollyrood Park has the highest point in Edinburgh. It's a pain to hike up to the top, much less run to it. To be honest, I'm not the most athletic of people. I'd rather watch a movie than take a run. Fiona puts my thoughts into words. "That sounds dreadful."

"I like to run," Asha defends herself. "It clears the mind."

"If my mind were any clearer, it would be empty," Fiona tells us with a grin.

"Yeah, Asha, I'm out too." Last time I went for a run with her I barely got half a mile before my legs cramped up and I felt like I was going to die. "I'll go for a walk with you, though, if you're ever interested."

"Okay, but what are we going to do tonight?" Fiona asks, reaching for another candy bar. "I brought some films."

"Anything scary?" I ask.

"Nope . . . romantic comedies."

"Sounds good," Asha says. She's always been a sucker for a good romance, even when we were little.

"Well, I just downloaded a movie called *Blood Dawn*." I pointedly ignore the fact that Asha looks like she just smelled something bad. "It's about vampires. . . ."

"Oh, I'd watch that," Asha says, relieved.

"Um . . . well, they're not exactly the sexy, eternal-love vampires . . . they're more like the rip-out-your-throat-and-eat-your-face vampires."

Asha's relieved look fades.

"Hey," Fiona cuts in, "as much as I love being scared out of my pants, how about we watch the rom-com first . . . then we can watch *Bloody Mess*."

"*Blood Dawn*," I correct her.

"That's what I said. And after that we can watch TV, because James McAvoy is on a chat show and I dinnae want to miss a minute of my future husband's dreamy, perfect face." She does this sigh thing and stares off into the distance. Asha and I glance at each other and laugh.

"Fine, then shove over," Asha says, moving onto the couch. "Give me one of those Yorkie bars," she says with a shrug. "Might as well enjoy myself."

"Should we order pizza?" I ask.

"Aye!" Fiona shouts. "Extra cheese, pepperoni, and sausage."

Asha makes a disgusted face. "Half that, half plain cheese?" I ask, and Asha gives me a grateful nod.

And when the pizza arrives and we all grab slices,

laughing and joking, I almost forget all the things that are wrong with my life.

I'm having trouble getting to sleep when I hear a key scrape against the door before it finally turns in the lock and my aunt stumbles into the flat. I get up from my makeshift bed of blankets on the floor.

"Heather! What are you doing up?" she asks loudly.

"Shhhh, Fiona and Asha are asleep," I whisper. We head to the kitchen and I let out a laugh as she slumps into a chair with a grin. "And you're drunk!"

"I am no' drunk!" she denies loudly. "But I am an adult whom . . . whom . . . ." She can't seem to remember what she was about to say. "You know what would be fantastic right now?"

"What?" I ask.

"Chips!" she shouts.

I laugh. "I think that can be arranged." There's a chip shop right on the corner that's open really late.

"Smashing!" she calls out. "Wake your friends and see if they want some too."

"As if anyone could sleep through that." Asha appears in the kitchen, Fiona trailing behind.

"Great. Join us for a midnight snack."

"More like a two a.m. snack," I correct Aunt Abbie.

"You seem well," Asha says, hugging my aunt.

"Better than well, she seems absolutely tip-top." Fiona also gives her a hug and they sit at the table while I run downstairs to the chip shop. When I return and put down the bundle of chips, my aunt yells, "Beautiful!" and we all dig in.

"I'm going to bed," Aunt Abbie declares when we're finished, wiping her chin with a napkin. "Dinnae wake me in the morning."

"We won't," we say in unison, which causes a fit of giggling.

Soon Fiona is back on the couch, snoring away. Asha and I get comfortable on the floor.

"Your aunt looks good," she says. "From what my father told me, I was afraid . . ."

I want to tell her about the chemo not working and how Abbie isn't doing very well, but I don't want to ruin the evening.

"Yeah, she doesn't seem sick at all."

Asha gives me a smile before rolling over, and soon the sound of her breathing is deep and even. I can't sleep, though; I have too much on my mind.

Not to mention the dread of what new horrors might haunt my dreams.

10

prudence

August 1, 1621
The Highlands

PRIMROSE AND I cross the threshold together, and Mam looks up from the table. It is brimming with plants and flowers, beautiful and fragrant. Before her is her grimoire. The book holds all her secrets. Da is to never see it, never to ken about it.

Mam smiles her broad, kind grin. "Sit, lassies. Your da is expected back tonight, so this is our last lesson for a while."

We eagerly go to the table, settling in on either side of Mam. I stare at the grimoire, so close all I have to do is reach out and touch its pages. But I stop myself. That book is full of magic. No' the magic of fairy tales, which are just made-up stories, but real magic. Magic that uses the power of herbs and flowers and nature. Magic that heals.

Still, my fingers ache to touch the book, each page painstakingly handwritten, each illustration drawn with care. I sit on my hands. One day the book will be mine, mine and Primrose's, but no' today. Today I have to listen and pay attention and no' let my thoughts wander, not like Primrose. When I pinch her and whisper for her to pay attention she says, "It isnae my fault I would rather be outside, the earth between my toes, the Highland wind in my hair."

"Primrose." Mam's voice snaps us out of our squabble. "You always have your mind in the clouds, lass." I beam, self-satisfied, but then she fixes her knowing eyes on me and I hang my head, chastised.

"Prudence, I want you to name this plant." She points to one on the table, a wildflower with fernlike leaves and creamy white petals. I reach for it and inhale the fragrance, syrupy and nutty.

"Meadowsweet," I say, placing it back on the table. Mam looks at me expectantly and I continue. "It treats fever and pain." I ken them all by heart, but Mam likes to test us to be sure. There's nothing worse than using the wrong ingredients in a physic. What is supposed to heal someone may very well kill them if used incorrectly.

She turns to Primrose, pointing to a different flower. "Saint Columba's plant," Prim says without hesitation. She also knows all the plants by heart. She wants to impress Mam. "Gives courage to the craven."

Mam's eyes are on me once again. She points to a flower that I have never seen before. "I cannae name it," I confess. "It doesnae grow around here, does it?"

"No," Mam confirms. "It comes from the continent . . .

it's anise. It prevents bad dreams." She hands it to me so I can familiarize myself with it, then gives it to Primrose, who studies it dutifully.

Satisfied, Mam next takes a bundle of cloth from the table and opens it, showing the contents to each of us in turn. "And what is this?"

"Belladonna," Primrose and I say together.

Mam nods. "Deadly nightshade. Poisonous. In small amounts it can be used to lessen pain."

She wraps the berries back up and puts them back on the table. "We should do something different today," she tells us, and my eyes snap to Primrose, who grins. We've been waiting for this for a long time. We've been waiting on magic.

Mam consults her grimoire and then takes a sampling of herbs from the table. She explains as she works how each flower, each herb, each ingredient, must be in perfect proportion. She drops them all in a bowl and crushes them with a pestle.

"Magic isnae about witches and fairies and ghosties," Mam tells us. "It's about pulling on nature's energy. It's about knowledge and intent." She rolls up her sleeve, revealing a scabbed gash that runs along the side of her arm from her wrist to her elbow.

"I cut myself when I fell on the hill the other day, and I dinnae want your father to ken." I grimace. Father gets angry over silly things sometimes. We've each felt his lash, Primrose more often than Mam or myself. She eyes me, wondering if I will try to correct Mam's use of *ken,* but I dinnae dare.

Mam takes the mixture from the bowl and dabs it on the middle of the wound. "Some women like to chant when they apply their salves," she tells us. "It helps them concentrate, allows them to focus their intent. But I have always found words distract my attention."

She looks from me to Primrose and back again. "This salve will heal a wound, no matter who applies it. It will clean and help the skin knit together, and in a week or so the scab will fall off, and in a few years the scar will fade. The magic," she says, "is what we add to the mixture. It is us. We pull energy from nature and channel it through ourselves. Few can do what we do."

She takes her apron and wipes her arm. Where once there was an uninterrupted gash, the wound is now in two parts, one near the wrist and one near the elbow. The middle is completely healed. I gasp.

Mam urges us to try, and Primrose and I each mix a salve. I apply mine to the lower part of Mam's arm; Primrose applies hers to the top. When Mam wipes them both off, the wound on the top is completely healed, as if she'd never hurt herself.

Primrose grins. Magic is easy for her. It isn't for me. The gash is still apparent near Mam's wrist, and actually looks a bit worse. It has begun to ooze, dripping blood into the bowl I've used to mix her salve.

My face tightens, and I know my expression is sour.

"I will try again, Mam," I tell her, grabbing the bowl. I'm embarrassed I've failed. I hate always being second best.

"No!" Mam screams, slapping the bowl from my hands.

Her look of shock echoes my own as she grabs me by the shoulders. "Dinnae ever mix blood into a potion. Do you ken?"

I nod, fear coursing through me. Mam turns to Primrose. "Understand?"

"Yes, but what if a wound is bleeding?" she asks.

She takes a few breaths. "Only accomplished healers can dress a bleeding wound with magic. There is power in blood. Remember what I told you about intent?"

"Aye."

"*I* can heal a wound without drawing on the magic of the blood, but you girls need to stay away from it altogether. That's why I waited a few days for my wound to scab."

"Why?" I ask. "Why cannae we use the blood, if it is so powerful?"

"Blood Magic is dark and shouldnae be trifled with," Mam snaps at me. "We draw power from nature, no' ourselves," she says quietly. "If you were to use your own life force to heal, where would that leave you? Blood Magic is used to harm, no' to help. Promise me that neither of you will ever try it."

"Aye, Mam," I say. Primrose just nods.

She tells Primrose to mix more salve while she cleans up the mess on the floor, wiping the blood from her arm. I sit and sulkily watch. I could have made another salve. I could have tried again. When Mam is ready, she applies the mixture and her whole arm looks as good as new. The lesson is over.

Primrose and I move the herbs to the shelf, putting each in its proper place. But she says she feels a little faint, so Mam has her take a seat.

"It drains you, doesnae it?" She strokes Primrose's hair and smiles. "Are you tired?"

"Aye . . . but mostly I'm hungry."

She grins and gives her one of the oat cakes that we oftentimes eat for breakfast. I stand near her, my chest tight, my expression pinched.

"Next time, it will work for you," she whispers, but I dinnae want to hear her encouraging words. I glare at her.

Mam gathers the grimoire and any ingredients that Da might find objectionable and bundles them in a linen bag. She carries them to the hearth and pulls out a stone on the bottom left corner. She places the bag inside and returns the stone.

I feel a rush of pride, knowing something that even Da doesnae. Sharing that secret with Mam and Primrose.

Mam goes out to milk the sheep, and I'm quiet as we clean the cottage and prepare the evening meal. Primrose isnae much help, saying that she is tired, so she has to stop and rest a lot, leaving me with most of the work. Her laziness doesnae improve my foul mood. I seethe, thinking of all the things that Primrose is better at than me. Why did she have to take this too? Da wouldnae like it.

"This is wicked, what we do," I say eventually. I want to irritate her, lessen her achievement. "It goes against God. Da would be angry with us."

"Dinnae tell Da," she begs. "Mam isnae bad. She helps people."

"And what of Blood Magic?" I ask.

"Mam said no' to do it."

"No' unless you know how," I say, trying to upset her.

It works. She stands and practically spits, "You dinnae say a word to anyone or . . . or . . . I will get a knife and use your blood in a potion. Mam said it would drain your life."

I'm shocked she's said something so horrible. "You would never."

"I would. I would punish you with Blood Magic if you tell a soul," she threatens.

My mouth snaps shut. Primrose fumes and goes to sit on our bed while I sweep the floor.

I let her sulk, still surprised at her passionate anger. She's never yelled at me like that before. Maybe it has something to do with the magic. Maybe I should tell Da.

I look over to her, her face so like mine, yet so not. I'll protect her, even from magic. I'll protect her, no matter what it takes.

11
heather

PRINCES STREET GARDENS is beyond packed. Even though it's overcast and misty, tourists are out in droves. I hide under the overhang of the adjoining mall, twenty minutes early to meet Robby.

My phone dings as I'm waiting.

Heather, my girl. How's bonnie Scotland?

Great, Dad. It's raining. I'm on Princes Street right now.

A pause.

You're not roaming the city by yourself, are
you?

I sigh. I've been wandering Edinburgh on my own since I was thirteen and my parents stopped coming for the summer. My aunt decided I was old enough not to make stupid decisions. I wonder how much of what she lets me get up to actually makes it back to my parents. Especially now.

I met this guy named Ewan and he convinced
me to go back to his flat, where we're going to
do some heroin and then start a rebellion to
rid Scotland of the English . . . or something.
He wasn't really clear on the details.

Smart arse

The rain stops and sun peeks out from behind the clouds and I make my way into the park. It's perfectly manicured, with flower beds bursting with color. It makes up the base of the hill, and there are trails that climb the steep slope up to the castle itself. I wonder if my camera is on one of those paths . . . not that it would be salvageable after the fall and the rain. I stare up at it for a long while before finding a people-less patch of grass, and debate whether to have a seat. The grass is still wet, and I don't want to walk around the rest of the day with a damp butt, but really, who am I trying to impress? Robby? Please.

My hoodie is already wet from my walk in the rain, so

I take it off, turn it inside out, and lay it on the grass, hoping it will keep my jeans from getting too soggy. As soon as I sit down, though, the sun comes out full blast. After a few minutes of people watching I lie back and close my eyes, soaking in the rays.

"Heather!"

My eyes fly open. A man in a kilt hovers above me, concern marring his handsome face. He knits his dark eyebrows together and I realize that I know him.

"Robby?" I ask, uncertain. He wears the Brodie Tartan, hunter green with a crisscross pattern of yellow and orange squares. Most Americans would think of this pattern as plaid, but in Scotland it's so much more than that. Each family has their own tartan, different colors in which they dress with pride. He also wears a gray shirt that reads EDINBURGH GHOST TOURS in gothic script.

"Who bloody well else would it be?" he asks, and I shake my head, lost for words. The sun is shining, but a chill runs through my body. I'm so cold I begin to shiver. "You're trembling, and your lips are blue." He kneels beside me, and close-up, I wonder how I recognized him at all. Gone are the baby-fat cheeks and acne. His face is lean, his jaw firm. Definitely not how he looks in his Instagram selfies.

He helps me up, and I notice how strong he is now. Wide shoulders frame his body, and he rubs my arms with his hands, trying to warm me. "You've gotten taller," I say.

He laughs. "Among other things." He drops his hands. "There, now you're the proper color. How do you feel?"

"Fine. Thank you," I say, suddenly self-conscious. I

realize there's a crowd of people gathered around us. I pull away from him and pick up my hoodie, my face hot.

"Great. Now that we've sorted out the high-maintenance American, we can begin. Ready for the tour, everyone?" he asks loudly, giving me a wink.

I roll my eyes. He's the same old obnoxious Robby.

Robby moves through the park and up to Princes Street. I follow along with the large crowd, only half listening as he goes on about this or that murder. It *is* cheesy, meant to spook the tourists with Edinburgh's sordid history. Robby was always "hamming it up," as my mother says, but now I can see that that quality I used to find annoying has been turned into something . . . not quite attractive, really, but he's become magnetic.

"Who here has heard of *The Strange Case of Dr. Jekyll and Mr. Hyde*?" We're paused in one of the stone alleyways between buildings that crisscross up the hill and through the Royal Mile. Everyone raises their hands. There are a few Australians in the group, a family of Japanese tourists, a German couple, and a group of Canadians who each wear a maple leaf pin on their shirts so they won't be mistaken for Americans.

We stand outside a pub as Robby explains that Robert Louis Stevenson based his tale on a well-respected Edinburgh tradesman named Deacon Brodie, who turned to a life of crime to support his gambling debts. I raise my eyebrows and Robby catches my look.

"I can assure you that despite our shared last name, this man has no relation to myself, although I cannae be completely sure, as he had several mistresses and fathered many illegitimate children." He gives me a wink. "By day he was a gentleman, but at night he was a thief and a cutthroat." We walk a little farther up the high street. "Deacon Brodie was hanged right here in front of forty thousand witnesses."

"Forty thousand?" someone repeats.

"There wasn't much for entertainment back in those days. . . . I guess it's the eighteenth-century version of *Pop Idol*."

We head back down the street, past shops that sell Scottish wool scarves and cheap kilts. There are also a ton of whisky specialty shops, and I remember I have to remind my aunt to go shopping for my dad one day, not that he would let me forget.

"Stay together, stay together," Robby calls out. "Let's keep nice and cozy so nobody gets lost." We stop in front of another pub, of which Edinburgh has no shortage.

"This is where the infamous duo of entrepreneurs, Burke and Hare, hatched their murderous plans." Someone next to me gasps and I can't help but smile. I think Robby's found his calling. "These body snatchers dug up freshly buried corpses and sold them to the medical college." He explains that when the supply didn't meet the demand, they decided to take matters into their own hands and make some new bodies, murdering at least sixteen people.

As we walk, Robby points out various historical sites and a pub that makes the "best haggis and tatties" in all of Scotland. We turn at the castle and wind down the hill as Robby explains that royalty hasn't lived within its walls for centuries, and before it was open to the public it was used to garrison soldiers. At the bottom of the hill we end up in a graveyard. A thrill of excitement goes through me, the same as when I'm watching a horror movie. It's the scary-but-safe feeling I love so much.

"Who here has heard of the black plague?" Robby asks. Everyone raises their hands.

"And who knows how many people died during the plague years in Scotland?" No one ventures a guess, and Robby continues. "About half the population. Whole families died off in a matter of days. In fact, if a building was known to be affected by the plague, it would be boarded up and the inhabitants would be left to rot, sick or no'." Robby was playing up his accent for the tourists. I'm starting to find him kind of charming, and then I shake my head. What am I thinking? This is Robby. I once saw him devour an entire tray of my mother's deviled eggs, which he then immediately puked up onto my shoes.

You can't unsee something like that.

"Though many died from the bubonic plague, a few recovered. They were then tasked with removing the bodies of those who had succumbed to the dreadful pox. These"—he motions at the gravestones around us—"are the lucky ones. Rich men and women who had family that could afford to bribe officials for a proper, Christian burial. Many more were no' so lucky."

As Robby continues his speech, I rest my hand on a gravestone. Its epitaph is indecipherable. So many dead. The coldness of the stone numbs my hand and a chill runs up my arm to my spine, causing me to shudder. I draw my hand away as a cool breeze blows across my back, and pull up my hood.

"How many of you are familiar with the Meadows?" Robby asks, and a few people raise their hands. "Right now it's a lovely park with a fun fair . . . a good place to bring the kiddies or to have a picnic. Four hundred years ago it was the site of a mass grave for plague victims."

Once again, a chill creeps through me.

"Moving on," Robby says, taking us up the hill toward the castle. I barely listen as he talks about the many ghosts that supposedly haunt its stone walls. We head back down to Princes Street, the tour ending in the gardens where it started.

"Another park with a dark secret," Robby tells us. "This area used to be a loch. At the height of the witch hunts of the seventeenth century, witches were put on trial. Their hands and feet were bound and they were tossed into the water. If they floated, they were proven to be witches and later burned at the stake. If they sank to the bottom, they were innocent and went to the heavens as good Christian women."

"Did many witches die here?" I blurt out.

Robby's dark eyes snap onto me. "Thousands. During the witch hunts, Scotland claimed more witches per capita than any other country. I guess we're a wicked lot," he says with a wink. "Now, thank you all for joining me on this tour. Dinnae forget to tip your guide."

I let Robby finish, looking at the gardens in a new light. Such horrible things happened here. My dream comes back to me . . . magic and witches and creepy children playing. Maybe I should stop watching scary movies, like my mom suggested.

"Heather." Robby comes up behind me. "What did you think of the tour?"

"Very informative. You're good at it."

He smiles, and for some reason my stomach dips. "And how's Alistair?" I ask.

"Fine. In St. Andrews with his girlfriend," he says. "Hey, there's a ceilidh next Friday. Want to come?"

"Isn't that like, a dance for old people?" I ask, a little sad at the news that Alistair now has a girlfriend.

"Come on, it'll be fun. Duncan and Asha are going, and I'm sure we can get Fiona on board. Say you'll come, Heather." He looks down at me, a half smile on his face, his dark eyes bright, and I have no choice.

"Yes," I say.

"Great!" He picks me up in a bear hug, spins me around, and sets me back down. "Now, I have an hour before my next tour. What do you want to do?"

"I'm not sure," I say, flustered. "I guess get a snack, and maybe go find a piper to listen to on the high street." During the festival there are always people playing the bagpipes for the crowd.

He laughs. "You're the only person I know who actually enjoys listening to bagpipes. I bet you even like haggis."

"It's not bad," I say. "As long as you don't think about what's actually in it. I'm not a huge fan of onions."

He laughs again. "But the sheep heart, liver, and lungs are perfectly fine."

I put my hands over my ears. "Not thinking about that . . . ," I singsong. I drop my hands. "Okay, I'll admit haggis is pretty gross when you consider what it is, but so are a lot of foods. I mean, I love honey, but I don't want to think of it as bee vomit."

"Fair enough." Robby smiles. "But chips are okay?"

"There is nothing disgusting about chips. . . . I mean, except for the whole being deep-fried part." Mentioning fried things makes me remember another Scottish delicacy.

"And while we're at it, maybe we can get a deep-fried Mars Bar."

Robby grins at me. "I think that can be arranged. Do you remember when you bet I couldn't eat five of them in one sitting?"

"Yes! You got three in and you got all pale and sweaty. I thought you were going to have a heart attack." I glance at him. The Robby standing before me looks so different from the silly, stubborn boy I used to hang out with.

"Still, I choked down those last two. It was a matter of pride."

"You totally did, but you had a stomachache for like, a week afterward."

"It was worth it, to win."

"And what did you win?" I ask. "I can't remember."

"I think you bet me a fried Mars Bar." He busts out laughing. He rubs his stomach. "I feel a little sick just thinking about it, actually. Not really a well-thought-out bet. I dinnae think I ever collected."

"Well, come on. I'll buy you some chips, at least. For old times' sake."

As we walk up the hill toward the Royal Mile, he takes my hand. We used to walk like this when we were children, until someone, probably Fiona, made fun of us. We haven't held hands for years. Now he holds my hand as if it's the most natural thing in the world. Maybe it is.

12
ḥeatḥer

MY VIDEO CHAT session with Dr. Casella goes okay. In spite of the time difference, I get to keep one of the time slots I had at Great Lakes; Monday at four p.m. It just means I have to speak with her at ten p.m. Scottish time. I tell her about my grandmother. About my aunt. About my parents not telling me that her cancer is back. I basically have an Aunt Abbie–sized rant. It feels good to get it off my chest.

At the end she asks some more questions about my grandma and the type of dementia she's suffering from. It leaves me wondering. Gram's always been kind of crazy . . . could that mean there's something wrong with me genetically?

Dr. Casella said in her psychiatrist way, "No, Heather, I'm sure you're fine. I just like to have as much information as possible." She leaned too close to the camera, so her head was too big on the screen.

After we say good-bye, I shut my computer, and sit back. Usually speaking with Dr. Casella makes me feel better, but tonight I feel worse.

I give Fiona a call. "What are you up to?" I ask.

"Working. . . . These fest hours are killing me. We're open until midnight for the late crowds. Oh, did I tell you? My mum actually hired a waiter."

"As in someone who isn't related to you?" I ask.

"Aye, he's here for the summer from Spain. He's dead cute."

"*Muy bien*," I say.

"*Muy sexito*," she replies.

I laugh. "I don't think that's actually Spanish."

"I dinnae care. He's fit, and has these lovely dark eyes. . . ." She pauses. "I'm on the phone!" she screams. Then, "Well, if they want bread, they can bloody well wait or get it themselves."

"I'll let you go," I tell her. "I'm sure you have hungry customers."

"Pigs!" she mumbles; then I hear her say, "I wasnae talking about you, lady."

I hang up the phone feeling much, much better. Then I hear Aunt Abbie coughing in her room, so I get up to bring her a glass of water. I'm glad I'm here for her, but I also feel horrible knowing I can't help her. I wish I could take away her cancer. I wish I could make everything okay.

It takes me a few days to work up the nerve to go see Gram again. I feel like a horrible granddaughter, avoiding her, but I don't want to see her like that, confused, lost to another time and place.

Aunt Abbie has a chemo session at the hospital, so I ride the bus with her, getting off at the senior care facility. We called ahead and the nurse said Gram was having a "good day," but I'm still anxious.

Inside the nursing home I make my way to the reception desk. "I'm here to visit Anne MacNair. I'm her granddaughter."

"I remember you," the receptionist says brightly. "You were here the other day with Abbie. How is she?" she asks, handing me a clipboard full of signatures.

"Fine," I say, signing my name and the time.

"Do you need help finding the room?" she asks.

"No, I remember, thank you."

I walk slowly down the corridor and pause at the door. Gram is watching a quiz show on her TV, shouting out answers with gusto.

She turns to me, and a wide smile breaks across her face. "Heather! How are you, love?"

I hug her, glad she knows who I am. It's just like last summer. Sometimes she would get confused, sure, but all you had to do was prompt her a bit and she'd remember everything.

"And where's Abigail?" Gram asks expectantly, offering me a crisp from the bag in her lap.

"I . . . um . . . she couldn't make it," I say, unsure if Gram knows, or even remembers, that Aunt Abbie's cancer has recurred. I take a crisp and gingerly nibble at it.

"Oh, aye, those dreadful chemo treatments," Gram tells me. "Sometimes the cure is worse than the disease."

So she does know. "Yeah, I'm worried about her, but I know she'll pull through."

"Of course she will. The surgery went so well. The chemo's just a precaution."

"Surgery?" I ask. Dr. Campbell said they couldn't operate this time.

"It's all right, love. Your parents probably dinnae want to tell you the details, but you're old enough to know. What are you now, nearly twelve?"

It takes me a moment to understand what's happening. My grandma thinks it's five years ago. She thinks it's the first time Aunt Abbie had cancer. I'm lost for words, but she fills the silence easily.

"It's barbaric what they put her through. There was a time when the women in our family were healers."

"Healers?" I ask. I don't remember there ever being a doctor in the family.

"Oh, aye. It was amazing what my own grandma could do with a few herbs and the right words."

I grab another crisp. "Sorry, Gram, I don't understand."

"But even in those times, as modern as Scotland was, there were suspicious people. I mean, no one would come out and say the word *witch*, but you know they were thinking it."

I nearly choke on my chip. "Are you saying your grandmother was a witch?" I ask, sputtering out crumbs.

"Oh dear. Have some tea," she says, offering me her cup. "Now, where was I?"

"You were talking about witches," I say, studying her.

"*Witch* . . . what a dreadful word. No' at all accurate. The women in our family have always healed with herbs, called upon nature to help us out a time or two. No' exactly the evils of witchcraft, if you ask me."

Gram just means our ancestors were midwives and medicine women, often accused of being witches back when people were ignorant and quick to hate a woman who was even a little different. I place the cup back down on the table.

"Oh, but that Blood Magic, that's another story. Unnatural, that."

"Blood Magic?" I repeat. "What's that?"

"Some nastiness you need no' concern yourself with. Just know that sometimes the women in our family go . . . wrong. It doesn't happen often, though. Either type. I mean, look at Abbie. I love that girl, but there isn't an ounce of magic in her."

Magic and witches again. I don't remember Gram being superstitious . . . and she always went to services at the Church of Scotland on Sundays. This must be a result of her dementia. She's just confused . . . except. If it weren't for the part she mentioned about the blood, I'd write off this whole conversation.

When I ask her to clarify, she closes her mouth tight and sort of sucks on her teeth, so I change tactics. "Gram, were any of the women in our family burned as witches, you know, back in the day?"

She stares over my shoulder. "Aye, it's a terrible business.

None of those women could have been witches, though. No' the kind that people ordinarily think of when they think of witches. You know, the *bad* kind."

I want to laugh and say, *As opposed to the* good *kind . . . like Glinda?* But my gram looks deadly serious. "And why not?" I ask.

She looks at me, crumbs on her chin and an eerie calm in her eyes. "Because, Heather, a Blood Witch cannae burn. A Blood Witch cuts her flesh and uses her own blood in her spells. A Blood Witch loses herself a little each time."

I exhale slowly, and the teacup that I placed on the table falls to the floor, smashing into a thousand pieces, causing me to jump out of my skin. "Oh my God, Gram," I say with a laugh. "I'm sorry. I must have put it too close to the edge."

"It was nowhere near the edge," she mumbles. "It was them who did it."

I get a broom and dustpan from the staff and clean up the shards. After that, all talk of witches and magic stops. I don't want to encourage her to talk about things that don't make sense, so instead I try to focus her on things that are real. We spend the rest of the time watching TV and chatting about events that happened five years ago. It's hard for me to remember all the things that were going on back then, but Gram acts as if it were yesterday. I guess in her mind it was.

Before I go she grabs my arm. "Now, dinnae go telling your dad I told you about witches. He's a man. He wouldnae understand."

"I won't," I promise. It would hurt him to know how far gone she is.

"And . . . you know if anything strange starts to happen, you can always talk to Sheena MacIntosh."

"I'm sorry, Gram. I don't know who that is." I assume it's another person from her past, or maybe someone she made up altogether.

"Of course you do. Aubrey's daughter. The one who married Calum Brodie."

"Mrs. Brodie? Robby's mom?"

"She's a talented one. It was clear early on that she had the gift, and Aubrey taught her well. Abigail never showed any promise, but maybe I should have told her more. I never really learned much myself. I was just frightened of . . . Well, never mind now."

"So I should talk to Mrs. Brodie?" I ask.

"Yes, dear, but no' right now. Maybe wait a few years. You have time yet. And it isnae a good time anyway." She lowers her voice and I lean in expectantly. "I hear she's getting a divorce," she whispers, as if it's taboo to say at full volume. I hold my tongue instead of saying yeah, that happened like, five years ago. Robby's dad had a midlife crisis and ran off to live in Germany with some woman he met while he was there on a business trip. Robby and his brother usually spend Christmas with him, and Robby sends me a postcard from Munich every year. Last year he sent one with a weird horned-devil-looking creature with a sack of children on the front, and he scrawled across the back, *Would Wish You Were Here . . . Except That I Wish I Wasn't.*

Gram turns back to the TV, and I kiss her on the head before leaving the room.

"Nice visit?" the receptionist asks as I walk by.

"Yes. Strange," I add.

"Oh, love, you have to get used to it. They don't always know what they're saying."

For the briefest of moments I almost believed everything my grandmother said. I almost thought our family had some long lineage of witches. I laugh as I wait for the bus. How can I be so naïve?

I'm feeling better about my strange conversation with Gram by the time I get home. Until I see my aunt.

She's on the couch, hugging a cleaning bucket. The treatment's been hard on her, and she's already puked up her lunch. I get her a wet washcloth to put on her head and tell her about my visit with Gram, about what she said about the witches.

Aunt Abbie laughs weakly. "She's always believed that otherworldy nonsense."

"Really? I had no idea."

"Well, you wouldnae. She talked to me more about it than your father. I remember once when I was about your age, actually. I sliced my palm while cutting potatoes, and you would have thought it was the end of the world. She accused me of doing something called Blood Magic and made me strip down so she could check my body for marks. After, she apologized and said it was all a joke. It was so strange. At the time I was angry with her. . . . Then, later, I just thought she was a little loopy. But now . . . I wonder if it was the start of her dementia, if even way back then her mind was failing."

"I don't know," I say, my own marks burning. With the one on my arm ruined, last night I started a new carving on my right thigh, and I can even now feel the itchy healing of a new scab. It's another spiral, carefully carved. For some reason, I felt compelled to draw it, to slice it into my skin. I want nothing more than to rip off that scab and make it bleed.

I make a lame excuse to my aunt about being tired, flee to my room, and pull out my computer. When I search for *Blood Witch,* there are a lot of video game and role-playing game references, but no real information. Finally, on a dinky-looking Scottish history website, I find a few paragraphs.

Though Natural Witches channel nature's energies to perform their magiks, Blood Witches use their internal power. While Natural Magik puts considerable strain on a witch, recovery is usually achieved fairly quickly. Blood Magik, on the other hand, drains more than just a Blood Witch's energy; it drains their very soul. Recovery happens more slowly, if at all.

That is why a Blood Witch becomes increasingly more cruel and ruthless, for they no longer have the thing that makes them human, especially when casting Blood Magik in quick succession. Their soul's energy does not have the time to replenish, creating a self-perpetuating cycle. A Blood Witch may not start off evil, but every time they perform the rituals using their blood, they sacrifice a bit of their humanity, allowing them to perform darker and darker magiks without qualms.

So my gram had the lore right. Blood Witches were supposedly bad because they gave up a bit of themselves every time they performed magic. My doubts come flooding back to me. What if Gram does know something about what's happening to me, something that I can't or don't want to understand?

I take a deep breath. I need to talk to Robby's mom. She'll be able to clarify what Gram is trying to tell me—or maybe she'll just tell me Gram's crazy and I'm a fool for listening to her. Or maybe we're both crazy. Maybe I have early-onset dementia. I rub my thigh.

Maybe I'm the one who's sick.

13

heather

ROBBY'S MOTHER'S SHOP isn't far. It's a tiny hole-in-the-wall place flanked by art galleries and restaurants. She sells "mystical Celtic objects" to tourists. I've always thought of her as sort of dippy, but now I'm not so sure.

I push open the door and am immediately assaulted by the scent of too much incense. I cough and Mrs. Brodie looks up from the cash register. She doesn't recognize me at first, but a split second later she grins. "Heather! Robert told me you were back."

She comes out from behind the counter and gives me a hug. She reeks of patchouli. She wears what she always wears: a loose, flowing dress that matches her New Age image. Her black-brown hair is streaked with gray. Long and wild, it hangs past her butt.

"What brings you by? Robert is working on the high street this summer, not here in the shop."

"I know, I just wanted to say hi." I browse the merchandise, crystals and necklaces for power. What am I supposed to say to her . . . my gram thinks you're a witch? She told me to come talk with you in case I'm one too? You know, the *bad* kind. It's just all too ridiculous, and I'm about to bolt when a silver necklace catches my eye. The charm is three half circles intersecting to form a larger, three-pronged symbol.

It's the mark I sliced into my hip.

"What is this?" I ask when I find my voice. My fingers itch to touch the charm, and I pick it up and hold it out for Mrs. Brodie to examine. "I mean, I know it's a Celtic knot, but does it have a certain meaning?" There are a hundred different Celtic knot symbols. I've always been drawn to this one, though, so much so that I've carved it into my flesh.

"Ahhhaye. That's a very powerful Celtic symbol. It's the Trinity knot," she explains. She takes it from me, tracing the pattern with her finger. "See how three semicircles intersect to form three points? But if you look closely, you can see it's all connected—it goes on infinitely."

"Oh . . . so Trinity like the Father, Son, and Holy Spirit?" I ask.

She smiles, handing the charm back to me. "Not necessarily. There are many meanings, all open to interpretation, but I think this really represents the mind, the body, and the spirit, three aspects that make up a human being."

I can feel her eyes on me as I stare at the knot.

"You know," she says, "before Christianity came to Scotland, there were the Druids. The term *holy trinity* had a different meaning, and was said to be used by . . . well, for lack of a better word, witches."

There it was again. *Witches.* I laugh, but it comes out loud and unnatural. "Witches?" I ask, making my voice drip sarcasm.

"It's all folklore, of course," Mrs. Brodie says. "Witches aren't real. But the Celtic legends tell us that the Trinity knot represented the three ages of life for a witch; the Maiden, the Mother, and the Crone—for witches were always women."

"Why? Why in the myths are witches women?"

"Well, that's just according to the lore. Traditionally, men have also been accused of witchcraft, but more often it was women. It was said because Eve was the beginning of all evil in this world. She conversed with the serpent, so only a woman was capable of such evil again, of contacting the devil and doing his bidding."

She laughs and I let out a breath I didn't know I was holding. She turns back to the counter and begins to tidy a tray of rings she must have pulled for another customer. "As if men aren't capable of evil! If you ask me, the world would be a better place without them!" She winks at me. "Except for my Robert and Alistair, that is. Now, their father, on the other hand . . ." She trails off. She pauses in her fiddling on the counter. "The myth of the witch revolves around women because women are more attuned to their natural surroundings."

"But what about Blood Magic?" I ask, looking for her reaction.

Her head jerks around. "Where did you hear about that? Not from Abbie . . ."

"No, from my gram. She mentioned something to me the other day. She . . . she doesn't really know what's happening around her anymore," I try to explain. "But she said that Blood Magic goes against nature."

Mrs. Brodie stares at me. "Aye, it does, or so the stories say. But Blood Magic is also the domain of women. Men . . . they often crave blood, but women bleed each month, whether they wish it or no'."

"Oh." My face wrinkles. "Right."

"Wince if you like, but there's power in blood. A witch who practices Blood Magic is a force to be reckoned with."

"Is it true that they would carve symbols into their skin?" I venture.

Mrs. Brodie's face twitches slightly. "And where did you hear *that*?"

"The Internet," I quickly say.

"Aye, Blood Witches would carve symbols of power on their bodies. That's where the devil's mark theory came from, but even that was distorted, as if having a mole or a wayward nipple truly marked you as a witch. Blood Witches carved their flesh and sacrificed their blood for power."

A shudder runs through me. "Yeah, but that's not real."

She smiles. "Depends on who you ask, I suppose." She

looks me up and down, studying me. Her eyes dart to the necklace in my hands.

"Keep it."

"Really?" It's expensive.

"Only if you promise to wear it."

I slip it over my head and tuck the charm into my T-shirt, the metal cool on my skin.

"I'll tell Robby you came by. He'll be pleased."

My face warms. "Thanks for the necklace, Mrs. Brodie."

"Please, dear, call me Sheena. And say hi to Abbie for me. Tell her I'll be by soon with that special herb for her nausea," she says. I raise my eyebrows, but she just shakes her head. "Nothing you need to concern yourself with."

Before I leave, I turn back to her. "You never said. . . . What did witches use the Trinity knot for?"

"It's supposed to help you obtain clarity," she tells me, her dark eyes shining. "A witch could use it to look into her past or her future, or to understand her present."

I leave the shop more confused than I entered. I'm also majorly creeped out. I feel like all eyes are on me. My paranoia still hasn't passed, even though it's been days since I've taken my medicine. Or maybe it's not just paranoia; maybe I am feeling something . . . more. Part of me wants to believe there is magic in this world, but Gram isn't exactly a reliable source, and to be honest, neither is Robby's hippie-dippy mother.

My phone buzzes with a text from Robby.

Mum just told me you stopped by . . . since ur out want to grab lunch w me? On my break soon.

94

I smile, pushing down my crazy thoughts. Robby is solid and real. I can just picture Sheena on the phone five seconds after I left, telling Robby I'd been there.

Sure, meet up at the Scott Monument? Grab food in New Town?

See you in fifteen.

Despite everything that's going on, just the thought of seeing Robby makes me happy.

Because, heaven help me, I have a crush on Robert Brodie.

That night I dream of murder.

14

prudence

September 4, 1624
The Highlands

THERE'S SOMEONE IN the cottage with Mam, one of the women from the village. I hope she'll leave soon. I hope Da returns and catches Mam at her evil ways.

I sit under the window, their voices carrying on the open air.

"I wish you would let me come and apply it," Mam tells the woman. "It will work better."

"Aye, but then my husband will ken I got it from you. I dinnae want to cause you and yours any trouble."

I hear him then. Da. He's back early. I knew he would be; I knew he would listen to me. He enters the cottage and there is a terrible ruckus. The village woman flees through the door, crying.

It sounds as if the devil himself is loose inside. Crockery smashes against the wall, and pieces fly through the window. They both scream, Da's words full of venom. Mam's cries are more guttural, and I cannae understand what she's saying. Da calls her evil, a witch, an unclean handmaiden of the devil. Da shouts long after Mam has gone silent.

After a while he leaves the cottage, finds me crouched under the window. He kneels next to me.

"You were right to tell me, Prudence." He holds out his arm and pulls me to him, holding me in a rare hug. "Where's your sister?"

"By the brook," I say quietly. I want to peek in the window, to look in on Mam, but I lack the courage.

"Go to the carriage. Now." His tone holds all his authority, and I obey him without question.

I walk slowly to the carriage, not daring to look back, and sit inside. After a long while, Primrose is thrust through the door. Her eyes and nose are red. She sniffles and eyes me hatefully. Da does not sit with us. He goes up front to drive the horses. We pull away from our home.

"You told him," Primrose spits out.

"I had to. It was the right thing to do."

"I hate you," she tells me. She's said those words to me before, but this is the first time I believe them. "I hate you and I will never forgive you for this." She wipes her nose. "Da says we're going to Edinburgh. That we are never coming back. That we're never going to see Mam again."

I nod, try not to cry. What have I done?

"What will she do without us?"

I think of the silent cottage and I do cry then. It hurts, and I wish I could take back what I did, but I cannae. All I can do is try to be good for Da. All I can do is hope that Primrose one day forgives me.

15

heather

I WAKE IN a cold sweat, my aunt at my side.

"Oh, love. Can I get you anything . . . water?"

"No, I'm fine," I tell her.

"Your father was so hopeful. He thought the night terror was an isolated incident. They thought the visit has been good for you."

"It has. That one wasn't so bad," I lie.

After I convince my aunt to go back to sleep, I change my pajamas and strip the bed of the soaked sheets. I pull my blanket around me and lie shivering on the bare mattress.

The Trinity knot was one of the first symbols I carved into my flesh. Mrs. Brodie said that witches used the symbol to see into the past. Is that what I could be doing? Dreaming visions of the past? If so, why? I can't do anything about the past. I can't save that woman. She's been dead for hundreds of years.

As have her twin daughters.

I sigh and close my eyes. I'll wait until Gram has another good day, one when she is truly present, and ask her to help me sort things out.

My dreams are trying to tell me something. Maybe they're warning me not to cut myself, to fight the compulsion. As if I could. But I did, for six whole weeks. The only thing that kept me going was knowing that once I got out of the Wellness Center, I'd be free to cut again. I waited and thought of blood to come.

I pull the blanket over my head, creating a cloth cave in which to hide. Why can't I just have normal thoughts? Normal problems? I close my eyes tight and try to think of nothing.

A thought that is not my own bounces through my head. *I will not let Prudence win. Not again.*

In the morning, I catch my aunt talking on the phone with my mother, telling her about my nightmare. I flash her a betrayed look before going into the kitchen and pouring myself some cereal. She thinks she's being quiet, but I can hear every word.

"I dinnae know. . . . I'm sure that's no' necessary. No.

She wouldnae tell me." After that I actually can't hear what she's saying. When she appears in the kitchen I give her another look, eyebrows raised.

"What did Mom have to say?"

She sighs. "She wants you to come home. She thinks you might need more help than your weekly sessions with Dr. Casella can provide."

I pause mid-bite. "She wants me to go back to Great Lakes?"

"No. Not exactly. Between the cutting and the new developments . . . she thinks you might be better spending the summer in . . . well, I dinnae know how else to say this . . . in hospital."

"Like, a mental hospital?" And I thought the Wellness Center was bad. I take a deep breath and put my spoon down in my bowl. "I mean, I have some serious issues, but I'm not crazy."

"No one thinks you are." She sits next to me at the table.

"If anyone is crazy, it's my mom if she thinks I'm going to fly home just so she can keep an eye on me."

"I talked her out of it," my aunt says. "Your father wasn't exactly on board either."

"Oh. Good." I pick my spoon back up, then immediately put it down again. "Thank you for telling me."

"Honestly, I dinnae want you to leave. And I dinnae believe you're nearly as bad as your mother thinks, but she's worried."

"She's always worried. I just can't believe she wants to have me committed. . . . No, I do believe it. She didn't want

101

me to leave the Wellness Center, and she didn't want me to come here."

"She's just worried about you. And she never said 'committed.'"

I tilt my head. "What does having me stay in a hospital against my will sound like to you?" At least at Great Lakes, there was some semblance of free will, and being there was completely voluntary. Theoretically, I could have walked out at any time. Not that I had a choice. My mom would have freaked and I never would have made it to Scotland. A lot of the girls there were like that. They stayed not to get help, but to appease their parents. They only wanted to get better so they could get back to their lives.

Aunt Abbie fiddles with the napkins on the table. "She wanted me to ask you . . . well, she thought you might tell me things you might no' feel comfortable telling her. You know, you can always confide in me."

"I'm not hiding anything," I lie.

She looks at me. "But you *can* tell me anything you want, Heather. I thought your mum needed to know about the night terror, but . . . if there was something else that you dinnae want her to know, I would try to help you as best I could."

I nod. "I know, Aunt Abbie."

She stands. "I'm going to call to check on Gram. . . . Why dinnae you skip visiting with her today and go have fun with your friends?"

"Okay." I push away my breakfast, no longer hungry. "Thanks again, Aunt Abbie. For calming Mom down, convincing her to let me stay."

"No problem," she tells me with a wink. "We MacNair girls have to stick together."

The night of the ceilidh, I'm weirdly excited to see Robby again, and I don't want to think about what that means. What I'm not so eager for is the actual dancing part of the ceilidh. Scottish dancing is complicated. It's also high-energy and requires a lot of stamina. I've only ever watched people dance at a ceilidh before. I've never joined in myself.

Before I head out, my aunt looks me up and down. "You are no' going to a ceilidh dressed like that."

"What?" I ask. I'm wearing jeans, but I put on a dressy shirt and nice flats. She grabs me by the hand and leads me into her room, mumbling that my father isn't doing an adequate job teaching me about Scottish culture. Even though she's basically insulting me, I can't help but smile that she at least has the energy to rant.

She rummages around her closet and pulls out a black dress bag. "Here it is!" She puts it on her bed. "This is vintage, so don't spill anything on it," she warns as she unzips the bag. "It was your grandma's, and then mine, and now I'm giving it to you."

She pulls out the contents and holds it up and I gasp. It's beautiful. The shift dress is slim with a large black belt at the waist and looks both vintage and modern at the same time. There are always variations on a family tartan, but this version of the MacNair tartan is one of the girlier ones. Rich pink and magenta squares are bisected with white and navy blue intersecting threads. The neckline is ruched, with a navy silk bow that ties at the left shoulder strap.

"Here, let me help you get into it," my aunt offers.

"No," I quickly say, a little too loudly.

She gives me a strange look.

"I . . . don't want you to see my scars. It's embarrassing."

"Please yourself," she says kindly, and leaves me to change in her room. I slip into the dress, and even though I can't do up the back on my own, I know it will fit perfectly. One major problem, though: it's sleeveless. I hold up my arm and look in the mirror. . . . What am I going to do about the mark I've carved there? Normally it wouldn't matter—I could keep my elbows pinned securely at my side—but Scottish dancing often requires you to throw your arms in the air. I grab a couple of bandages and layer them over the wound. This will have to do. At least the bandages are sort of the same color as my skin, and maybe the dance hall will be dark. If anyone notices I can say I cut myself shaving. No, that's lame. Maybe that I had a mole removed. Yeah, still lame, but better.

I slip on my flats, grab my purse, and find my aunt to do up the back of my dress, which incorporates buttons instead of a zipper. "You look lovely." She sounds as if she's about to cry. She turns me around and takes me in. "Fits like a glove. You know, your grandmother's grandmother made this dress for her."

"The witch?" I ask without thinking.

My aunt looks confused. "Did Mum tell you that? She always told me that her gram was a lovely woman. Not a mean bone in her body."

"Maybe I got it wrong," I say.

"That is until she got really old. Then she went a little crazy and tried to hitchhike to the Highlands. She tried to steal some bloke's car whilst wielding a butter knife."

"Another family member who went crazy-cakes? Not exactly comforting."

My aunt laughs. "We MacNairs lucked out on the gene front. We've got a history of mental illness and cancer—and dinnae forget the heart disease." My grandfather Michael MacNair died of a heart attack at the ripe old age of forty-five.

"Great. No offense, Aunt Abbie, but can we talk about something else? My friends are going to wonder why I've suddenly become suicidal."

"No' funny, young lady. But you're right, I shouldnae have brought it up." She grabs her phone off the table. "Let me take a picture to send to your parents and then you can be on your way." She takes some snaps as I grin, trying to look as happy as I can. I want my mom to see I'm okay, not at all in need of medical attention. When she's satisfied with the pictures, Aunt Abbie walks with me to the door, slipping me a few bills.

"I promised your mum I'd escort you to and from the dance, but I figure you'll be fine if you take a cab," she tells me. "Be safe."

I give her a hug. "I will."

I type the address Robby gave me into my phone to get directions. It's in the area called Haymarket, so I hail a cab to get there. Normally, despite my mom's wishes, I'd just walk, but I have a feeling I need to conserve my energy.

When I spot Robby and Duncan waiting outside, I'm glad my aunt made me change. They're each wearing kilts in the family tartan, as well as jackets and bow ties, Scottish formal dress.

Asha is there too, and though her family doesn't have a tartan, she wears a cute black A-line dress with a ribbon of Duncan's family tartan tied around her waist, a deep purple with hints of white and gray. I always sort of thought Duncan was kind of cute, in a tall and gangly way. I actually liked his long, messy blond mane of head-banger hair. With it short, though, I can see why Asha suddenly noticed him. Clean-cut is definitely more her type.

She spots me getting out of the cab and waves. "Heather, you look smashing!"

"Thank you. You look amazing, all of you," I say, catching Robby's eye, and blush. I'm strangely out of breath. I fiddle with the Trinity knot necklace, tucking it into the front of my dress.

"Where's Fiona?" I ask.

"Inside, with my mate Craig," Duncan tells me. "Fiona refused to come if she was the fifth wheel of our double date, so I invited a friend for her."

"It's not a date," I say at the same time as Robby, and I can feel my face once again warm. I quickly add, "We're just friends."

"Really?" Duncan asks. "Then he talks about you much more than is healthy." Asha gives him a look and elbows him in the side. "What?" he asks with a grin. "It's true."

"Thanks, Duncan," Robby says, avoiding my gaze. "That was helpful. Now if we're done embarrassing me, perhaps we can go inside?"

He holds open the door and we walk into a ballroom of organized chaos. Scottish country music is a lot like bluegrass, with upbeat rhythms and lively fiddles. This band is a modern version, complete with electric guitar and keyboard. The rhythm is kept on a large, round hand drum.

"Is everyone in Scotland here?" I ask as we push our way through the crowd. The dance floor is filled with kilt-clad men and women in their best "dancing" dresses. It makes me think of an older time, a time before Scotland was "tame."

"My tour company throws a ceilidh once a year," Robert leans down and tells me. "Mostly it's the people who work for them and their families." He leads us to a table to the side, where Fiona sits with a boy, chatting excitedly. She's wearing a short green dress that shows off her long legs, and she holds a glass of amber liquid. She takes a few gulps before she spots us.

"Heather! Asha!" She hugs us and we sit. "This is Craig. He's eighteen and said he'll buy us beer." She winks at him.

"Hi." Craig gives us an uncomfortable smile. "She actually just swiped my pint, but I guess I can get drinks for you guys. . . ." He looks to Duncan.

"Um, thanks, but no thanks," Asha says immediately. "My parents would kill me if they thought I'd been out drinking. They'd never let me leave the house again."

"That's me out, then, too," Duncan says, giving Asha a sweet smile.

"You're no fun!" Fiona says, taking another gulp and

mumbling, "Whipped already," under her breath. "What about you, Heather?"

I feel a bit put on the spot, so I just shake my head. Robert leans down and whispers to me, "If you want to have a drink or two, I'll make sure you get home okay."

"No . . . it's just that my aunt pretty much lets me do anything I want when I'm here. I don't want to mess that up. Especially if my parents found out . . . my mom would go ballistic."

He nods, and I wonder if he thinks I'm lame. Whatever. He's been un-dorked for all of five seconds and—

"Let's dance," he says with a grin, pulling me onto the dance floor.

Scottish dancing is a lot like square dancing . . . with kilts instead of cowboy hats. There's even a person calling out the moves over the music. At first I'm scared I'll misstep. Robert drags me into a group of four other people and we form a large circle, and suddenly we're galloping around the circle like crazy people. When the caller tells us to stop, we each grab a partner and link arms and fling each other around. By the end of the first dance I'm sweating, out of breath, and having the time of my life.

"Ready for another go?" Robby asks me, panting slightly.

"You bet your sweet Scottish ass I am," I tell him with a grin. This time *I* pull *him* onto the dance floor.

"Oh . . . it looks like she's going to finally get it out. Wait. . . . Wait for it. . . . There she goes!" Robby shouts as

Fiona vomits on the sidewalk. He walks to her where she's bent over and puts a hand on her back. "You all right, love?" he asks kindly.

"I'm fine." She pushes him away. She stands up and wipes her mouth. "Better now, actually."

Craig bailed halfway through the dance when it was clear Fiona was only interested in him for his legal-to-buy-alcohol status. But by that time, Fiona was already blitzed. Asha and Duncan left a little afterward to keep her curfew. I took it upon myself to get Fiona home safe and sound, and Robby came along because, well, he's Robby and a good guy.

"Fiona, I love you," I say, standing back slightly. "But I really need you not to puke on me tonight."

Robby gives me a look.

"What? This dress is vintage," I say. Then laugh. "And also, I try to avoid being puked on as a general rule."

"Yeah, she got a little on my shoes with that one," Robby admits. "Let's get her home quick."

Fiona does seem better after she vomits, and is able to walk without our support. We were going to hail a cab but thought better of it when she started to look as green as her dress. I didn't want to inflict a puked-in car on some unsuspecting cabbie, or be in an enclosed space when she finally erupted.

Fiona's family lives in a flat above their café. It's not late, only about ten-thirty, and the café is open and packed. Her mom is super-permissive, but still, I think it's best to avoid her family at this point. I take the keys from her and help her upstairs. I lead/carry her to her bed. After that I get her a

glass of water and her small garbage can to puke in if necessary. She's snoring before I even leave the room.

Downstairs, Robby is waiting for me. His mom has a
small house in the New Town part of Edinburgh. Since we
live in completely opposite directions, I assume we're going
to part ways, but instead he grabs my hand and starts to
walk me toward my aunt's place.

"Don't you want to get home?" I ask.

"And leave a damsel alone in the night?"

"Sexist much?" I say. "I'm not a damsel. Besides, I can
catch a cab."

"Let's walk. It's nice outside."

It is nice. The night is warm and clear. He starts to walk
toward the Meadows and the shortcut home, and for a moment I pause, remembering my weird panic attack and my
near fall at the castle afterward. Robby misreads my hesitation and drops my hand.

"Unless . . . you'd rather be alone."

"No . . . it's just . . ." I eye the Meadows. There are still
people out, the carnival in full swing, rides lit up like fire-
works.

"Come on, there's nothing to be afraid of." He grabs my
hand again and pulls me forward. When my feet touch the
grass I brace myself for a horrible reaction, but none comes.
Instead, I get an eerie feeling of being followed, but when I
turn around, there's nobody there.

We walk on the soft earth in silence, until Robby starts
to hum a tune . . . then starts to sing in a strangely hyp-
notic voice.

"Oh, my love is like a red, red rose . . . that's newly sprung in June."

I roll my eyes and his voice gets louder. He always used to do stuff like this when we were kids, trying to desperately grab attention.

"Oh, my love is like the melody that's sweetly played in tune."

He hums a bit more and winks at me, and then he gets really loud, belting out each word until a crowd gathers. Once a ham, always a ham. He actually pulls my hand up and puts it on his chest.

"As fair art thou, my bonnie lass, so deep in love am I, and I will love thee still, my dear, till a' the seas gang dry!"

"You are such a dork," I tell him as he takes a long sweeping bow to the gathered crowd. He gets a nice round of applause.

"What? A little Robbie Burns is perfect on a moonlit night." He grins at the dispersing crowd.

"Does anything ever embarrass you?" I ask as I pull him across the park, toward the safety of my street.

"Let's see. . . . Once a girl called me a dork in front of about twenty people. That was pretty rough." He grins. "But it happened ages ago, a whole three minutes, so I'm actually over it now."

I sigh as I reach the building for my aunt's flat. "Well, this is me," I say wistfully. I don't want the night to be over, but I don't have a choice. It's not like I'm going to invite Robby up for a make-out session. We actually have kissed once before, when we were kids. My face goes red at the memory.

"Do you remember?" he asks, as if reading my thoughts, "when we stood right here . . . no, wait . . ." He takes my shoulders and moves me a few feet over, into a shadowy spot under the overhang, "and we kissed?"

I laugh nervously. "We were like, thirteen." It was the first summer I was here without my parents. It was amazing to have all that freedom.

"Yeah, and we'd just gone to some zombie film . . . no, wait, let me correct that . . . you dragged me to some zombie film, refused to share your popcorn with me, and then blathered on about Alistair the whole way home."

"I don't know if that's entirely accurate . . . ," I lie.

"And . . ." He leans in, his face inches from mine, his hand resting on my shoulder. "You were worried that the first time you kissed Alistair wouldn't be *magical* because you didn't know how to do it properly . . . so you nearly jumped me, right here in the entryway."

I'm feeling a bit light-headed, and I let out a small breath. "As I recall, you were a more than willing participant." I swallow, hard.

He smiles and leans in even closer. His hand reaches up and he sweeps a stray lock of hair off my face and puts it behind my ear. "I'd like to do it again," he says softly.

"What?" I ask breathily.

"See another film with you, of course," he says with a roguish grin.

"Robby, you are such a jerk." I push him away.

He laughs. "What did you think I meant?"

"Go away," I say as I get out my keys and unlock the front door.

"I'll kiss you if that's what you want," he says loudly. "At least this time you won't taste of popcorn and Maltesers."

I turn back to him. "Not in a million years, Robert Brodie," I say, flustered.

"We'll see, Heather," he tells me, taking a step back. He does a kind of good-bye salute and turns on his heel, humming his song. As I go inside and shut the door, my heart is beating out of my chest. I can just make out his voice singing "My love is liiiiiiike a reeeeed, red rose" as he disappears into the night.

16

primrose

April 20, 1629
Edinburgh

I CAN SMELL his scent on my clothes as I hurry along the dark street. I will have to change and wash before Father gets home. The walls of the city close in on me. After dark is the only time he can meet. I cannae help but smile. *Love*. It's such an inadequate word. I don't just *love* him. I adore him. I worship him. I want to consume him. I want to crawl inside his skin. When I am with him I feel on fire, as if my blood will burn through my flesh. It is at once terrifying and exciting.

I want to say his name. *Jonas*. I want to yell his name. *Jonas*. I want to sing it—*Jonas, Jonas, Jonas*.

But I cannae. I must remain silent for now. Nobody knows but us. We are to be married, but my father would have my hide. If he knew, he'd lock me up, or send me to the nuns. He'd never allow me to marry a Jew.

But these labels—Jew, Catholic, Protestant—that mean so much to so many mean nothing to me. My religion is the earth. My soul belongs to nature, to Scotland. And my heart belongs to him. Jonas. Is this how my mother felt about my father? Was her love not enough to melt his cold heart?

Prudence knows there is something amiss. She has left off her questioning for now, for she has come down with some illness. I hope she stays ill for days. I hope she is bed-ridden and I can have my moments of stolen bliss with Jonas go on until we elope.

My face heats at the thought of him. I know what we do is supposed to be wicked, but all I feel is the good of it. All I feel is love.

17
heather

I STEP ONTO the short well-kept grass, walking slowly. I take the path that cuts straight across the Meadows, where Fiona's family's café sits, nestled in a tall, modern building across from a much more imposing Gothic university one. Out of the corner of my eye I see a figure in the shadows, but when I turn my head, it's gone . . . if it was ever there in the first place.

Not for the first time, I debate whether I should tell anyone about my increasing sense of paranoia. I don't want my friends to think I'm a freak, and I don't want to put that worry on Aunt Abbie. I can't tell Gram or my parents. My mom would probably insist I get on the next flight home.

Dr. Casella is the obvious solution, but . . . I don't really want to.

My phone rings and I check the screen and sigh.

"Hey, Mom."

"Hi, Heather, I'm just checking in. . . ." My mom pauses, listens. "Where are you?"

"Crossing the Meadows, going to have a snack at Fiona's," I say without thinking. I should have just told her I was at Aunt Abbie's flat.

"You're not by yourself, are you?" she asks. "I don't want you walking around without Abbie."

I roll my eyes. "I'm fine," I say. "I'm not going to make Aunt Abbie escort me everywhere. She can barely get out of bed some days."

"Then maybe you should keep her company at home." Yeah, that would be my mom's dream come true, me as a shut-in. What's the point of traveling halfway around the world to be cooped up in an apartment all day? Besides, Abbie would hate me constantly hovering over her.

"Hey, Mom, I gotta go. Some guys just pulled up in an unmarked van. They say if I go with them I can have all the candy I want. And a puppy." Sometimes my smart-ass-ness diffuses my mother's worry—at least, it did before this summer. Now all she does is worry.

"That's not funny, Heather," she says, her voice going up an octave. "You are thousands of miles away in the middle of one of the biggest festivals in Europe. There are a million people crawling the streets, and any one of them could be a weirdo."

"Well, I'm here now," I tell her. "Unless you want me to turn around and go home unescorted across a park full of potential weirdos." She's silent, and I think I may have gone too far, but after a few seconds she exhales loudly.

"Just say hi to Janet and Doug for me. And in the future I don't want you to go out on your own."

"Sure thing, Mom," I say, though I have no intention of following her orders. I toss my phone into my bag and push open the door to the Celtic Goddess Café. It's packed, though it's past lunchtime. That's the festival for you.

I spot Fiona's mom running around like a crazy person, and her stepsister, Mary, jotting down orders.

"Hey, Mary," I call out across the restaurant. Mary glances up, not recognizing me. Her dad only married Fiona's mom a year and a half ago, and she's a little kid, so it's not like her not remembering me hurts my feelings. "Where's Fiona?"

She nods over her shoulder and turns back to her customers. I wonder how Fiona's mom gets around the child labor laws. Fiona's been working at the café since she was eight.

Fiona's sitting at a small table in the corner, her head in her hands. Even her curly red hair seems limp and tame. I slide into the seat across from her.

"Shouldn't you be working?" I ask. "You look absolutely awful, by the way," I say.

She winced. "Please, dinnae talk so loudly." Fiona catches Mary's arm as she walks by. "Fetch me a cup of coffee, would you?"

"Sure, Fifi." Mary grins. She idolizes Fiona, though they have nothing in common.

"And dinnae call me Fifi. I'm not a bloody poodle."

Mary turns to me. "And you . . . I know you . . . ?"

"Yeah, it's me, Heather," I say. "We met last summer."

"Oh, right. The American. What can I get you?"

"Cup of Earl Grey with honey . . . and some caramel sponge cake."

"It's not vegan," she warns. She points at the menu on the table. "Only items marked with a green *V* are vegan."

Fiona makes a growling noise. "Does she look bloody vegan?" she snipes. Mary backs away with a hurt look. Fiona's face softens. "Look, sorry, pet. I'm just not feeling well today."

Mary grins again. "It's okay, Fifi. I'll get you your coffee right away."

"What?" Fiona asks when I give her a look. "She's a pest."

I shrug. "She seems to be a big help to your mom."

"Yeah, no kidding. I think that's half the reason Mum married Doug . . . adding one more free waitress to the family."

Mary brings our drinks and cake and puts some scrambled eggs in front of Fiona. "Janet said to make you eat this and then you have to get off your arse and stop your moaning because she needs you to do some actual work today."

"Tell Mum I said thanks," she says sarcastically.

Mary eyes the eggs, a disgusted look on her face. "You know, that's the embryo of a chicken."

Fiona takes a heaping forkful and puts it in her mouth. "Mmmmm, embryo," she says with a big grin. The Celtic Goddess has a lot of vegan and vegetarian options, but it also has plenty of meat dishes, all free-range organic. Fiona once told me her mom, as much of a hippie as she is, didn't think the café could survive if it went straight up meatless.

Fiona drinks her coffee and picks at her eggs while I wolf down my cake. After she eats she offers me a small smile. "Thanks for getting me home last night."

"What are friends for?" I grin. "Robby helped more than me. He even held your hair back while you puked," I teased.

Fiona makes a face. "Yuck. Sorry. Hey, what's up with you and Robby, anyway?"

"What do you mean?" I ask, my face reddening at the thought of Robby and our almost-kiss.

"He couldn't keep his eyes off you, and you danced with him all night."

"I was having fun."

"I bet." She grins. "Well, the next time Robby carries me to my room, tell him he can just stay the night for a cuddle . . . ha!" She screams, pointing at me.

"What?"

"The look on your face. You like him."

I sigh. "I don't know. Maybe I do."

Fiona flashes a triumphant grin. "I knew it. Before, when Asha said there was something there, I thought she was just imagining it. She's been so gaga over Duncan and wants everyone to be in loooooooove. But now I totally see what she meant about you two."

"If . . . ," I say, "and this is a *huge* if," I stress. "*If* I like

Robby, I don't think I could date him. We've been friends for so long. It would be strange."

Fiona shrugs. "Just go for it, Heather. Let him know how you feel. Also"—she raises her eyebrows—"have you seen how hot he's gotten? Who'd have thought our fat little Robby would get so fit? You'd be crazy not to jump for a chance at that. If I thought he was at all interested, I would," she says wistfully. I narrow my eyes and she quickly adds, "But I really wouldn't ever because, you know, we're friends and that would just be wrong."

I laugh, and Fiona's mother appears suddenly at our table. "Hello, Heather," she says, her eyes on her daughter. "Lovely to see you."

"Hi, Mrs. Darrow."

"Fiona, we're swamped. I dinnae mind if you go out and have a little fun, but you've got to get yourself together the next day to work. Mary cannae do it all by herself. . . ."

"Okay, Mum," Fiona says with a sigh. She stands, gathering her plates. "I feel better now."

Her mom grabs a handful of hair, yanking it playfully. "I'd appreciate it if you told Mary what a good job she's doing. It would mean the world to her."

"Okay, okay." Fiona flashes me a grin. "See you later, Heather."

"Bye," I call as Fiona's mom turns to me.

"And how are you, love? How is Abbie holding up?"

"Good. The chemo is hard, but we're hopeful."

"Tell her to stop in if she's up for it. Sheena Brodie and I are collaborating on a holistic anticancer regimen of medicinal herbs and organic foods."

"I'll tell her," I say, standing so that paying customers can have my seat.

"And how is your grandma?" she asks, following me toward the door.

"Good, good. The home really was the best choice."

Her eyes drop to my Trinity knot necklace, then snap back up to my face. "Did your grandmother give you that?" she asks quietly.

"No." I almost forgot about it. "Mrs. Brodie, I mean, Sheena did. I saw her at her shop and she said I could have it." I touch the cool silver. "Is something wrong?"

"No. It's a lovely necklace." She hesitates, then smiles. "All right, love, take care of yourself."

"Thank you. I will," I say as I walk out onto the sidewalk. I think Mrs. Darrow is still watching me from the doorway, because I get this creepy feeling down my spine, but when I turn to look back, she's gone.

18

heather

THE NEXT TIME I see Gram she knows exactly who I am. The nurse is in her room, readying her for her daily walk, and I offer to take her. We head outside; the grounds aren't enormous, but there's a pretty garden and a nice path lined with benches. Gram wants to sit on one of the benches, and she asks me a million questions about what I've been up to, school and my life.

After a while I realize I'm starting to lose her. She seems unfocused and asks who I am.

"Heather, Gram. I'm Iain's daughter. Remember?"

"Oh, of course. I wanted to talk to Iain about the property in the Highlands. I dinnae want them selling it after I'm gone. It's been in our family for hundreds of years."

"What property?" I ask.

"You know, the cottage, Abigail. The one we'd bring you to when you were little so we could spend a few days in the country."

"No, Gram, it's me, Heather. Not Abigail."

"Of course, Heather. I get confused sometimes."

"I know." I put my hand on her arm. "It's okay, Gram. So, who used to live in the cottage?"

"What cottage, dear?"

"The one in the Highlands," I say patiently.

"Oh, no one for years and years. It was built . . . let's see, four hundred years ago? For a while it just sat up there, forgotten, falling apart. But then my great-grandmother had it restored. They were able to keep most of the original foundation and built around the bones of the place . . . but even those enhancements were made ages ago. It's quite the relic. Maybe you'll fix it up again. I'd like that." My grandmother shivers slightly.

"Are you cold?" I ask, wishing I'd brought a sweater for her.

"Aye, Abigail. Let's go back inside."

I nod, not bothering to correct her, and help her up. My grandmother is disappearing little by little and there's nothing I can do about it. I try not to cry as I walk her back to her room, even though my heart is breaking. The Gram I know will soon be gone.

Blood drips down my thigh as I slice through my skin. The release makes me gasp. I work on the mark on my hip, slowly recarving the symbol, the one that hangs around my neck. I can focus for hours, slowly cutting the pattern in my flesh.

After a while, the need passes and I put the knife down. I stare at the symbol etched in my skin and tears well up in my eyes. Why do I cut myself?

Ashamed, I clean and bandage the wound, flushing the bloody tissues down the toilet. I return to my room and lie on the bed, crying softly. What is wrong with me?

The next time I Skype with Dr. Casella, I try to explain to her how I feel like I'm two different people sometimes. The Heather who likes to have fun and be with her friends, and the Heather no one knows. Someone dark and twisted.

"But they're both me," I tell her, not looking at the computer screen, afraid of what she'll say.

"Heather, what you're describing sounds normal. At one time or another, everyone feels torn between two parts of themselves. I have to ask, though, have you ever lost time? Not known where you were or what you were doing?"

"No, nothing like that. I'd tell you if I had, I promise."

"Okay, I believe you. You're just under a lot of stress. Have you been taking your medicine?"

"I took my meds while I was in the Wellness Center, but when I started having the freaky nightmares, I stopped," I admit, slightly ashamed.

"Thank you for being honest with me. I'd actually like to write you a new prescription for antianxiety medicine. I'll have to speak with your parents about it."

"My mom thinks there's still something wrong with me."

Dr. Casella nods. "You mother expressed her concerns to me. About the night terrors."

"About having me committed?"

She tilts her head. "And how do you know about that?"

"Aunt Abbie told me."

"I did speak with your mother about that, and I explained to her that placing you in a facility against your will at this point wouldn't be prudent. You did wonderfully at the Wellness Center and seem to be committed to healing. I'll make sure she understands the ramifications of what she's advocating. I'll also always be here for you, Heather. I just want what's best for you . . . even if it means disagreeing with your parents about your course of treatment."

"Thank you, Dr. Casella. Do you think this antianxiety medication will help?"

"Yes. If your parents approve, I'll write the prescription in the morning. You should be able to pick it up at a pharmacy near you in the afternoon. My office will email you and let you know. But you have to take it. Every day."

"I will. I promise. Thanks again, Dr. Casella."

"No problem, Heather. Speak with you next week."

I turn off the computer with a strange mixture of relief and fear. Dr. Casella is in my corner, but what if she knew what I really thought? What I really do? What would she do if she knew the truth?

I'm not better at all.

19

heather

"ROBBY, IF YOU don't tell me where we're going, I'm turning around and walking home."

"Five more minutes, Heather, I promise," he says with a grin, grabbing my elbow and pulling me along. When he called asking me to come out with him tonight, I assumed we'd be with a group. But when he showed up at my door all tight lipped and mysterious, I knew he was up to something else.

"It's late. I have to get back soon," I warn. He's wearing jeans and a crewneck sweater, and I have to admit, he looks good. We went for dinner at an Indian restaurant and walked around the city, checking out the street performers.

"I told your aunt we'd be back late." He stops suddenly. "Here we are."

I look around at the crowd of people, then at the building behind them: an old theater. "Are we going to a movie?" I ask.

He grins. "Not just any film. The Scottish premiere of"—he pauses for dramatic effect—"*The Last.*"

My mouth drops. "Shut up." *The Last* is the biggest movie of the summer. "How did you score tickets?"

He shrugs. "Someone gave my boss a pair and he said I could have them. Well, actually, after I heard he had them, I went to his office and begged. I even offered to work the dreaded early shift. People on morning tours just dinnae tip. Why is that?"

"I don't know," I laugh. "But . . . I thought you hated scary movies."

"*Hate* is such a strong word . . . more like I loathe them with a fiery passion."

"Okay . . . then why are we here?"

"Because you love them, dummy," he says, shaking his head.

"That was awesome," I say. We're back at my aunt's place, standing under the overhang. Robby holds my hand, stands close. I tilt my chin up. He's so near, I can see stubble on his chin. When did he start to shave? The only time I feel like a normal person is when I'm around him.

Before I know what I'm doing, I lean forward. He smells so good. I mean to kiss him, for real this time, but he pulls away.

"It's late, huh?" he asks, his voice strained.

"Yeah, I was just thinking that too. I have to get upstairs. I . . ." I go for the door. "See you later, Robby." I give him an awkward pat on the shoulder.

"See you later," he says, backing away quickly.

I head up the stairs and find my aunt awake on the couch. "Couldnae sleep," she tells me. I collapse next to her and rest my head on her shoulder.

"How was the movie?" she asks. Robby must have told her where we were going.

"Confusing," I say.

"Hmmm, it got good reviews."

"I'm going to get some sleep." I lean over and kiss her. "Shout if you need anything."

"I will. Oh, your mom called me."

I stop at my doorway, turn. "And . . . what's her problem this time?"

"She doesn't want you wandering the mean streets of Edinburgh by yourself."

I grimace. "Sorry if I got you in trouble."

She lets out a soft laugh. "Heather, I'm a grown woman. I'm not in trouble."

"So . . . am I still allowed to wander?" I ask hopefully.

She sighs. "I love having you visit every year, love having you here. I would never do anything to jeopardize that, or to put you in danger." I nod, waiting for her verdict. "Your mother has always been a bit overprotective, and when she walked in on you at the beginning of summer . . . let's just say she wants to keep you safe at all times. But honestly, Heather, you're old enough to take care of yourself. You have been for a very long time. Even if you do have—"

"Issues," I say.

"You've always been a very responsible girl. I guess, until you prove otherwise, I'm going to assume you're still that same responsible girl, with a few issues thrown in."

I let out a relieved breath, one I hadn't realized I was holding. I've gotten used to having my freedom here. "Thanks, Aunt Abbie." At least she thinks I'm the same person.

"But . . . maybe let's not be so snide to your mother and rub her face in the fact that she cannae hover over you while you're here. Especially in light of her newest idea about your course of treatment."

"No, you're right. She just . . . she just gets on my nerves."

She smiles. "When I was your age, your gram drove me absolutely mental. I thought she was so clueless." She shakes her head. "It won't always be like this, though. I promise."

"And I promise I'll be smart and play nice." I notice a travel guide to Australia on the cushion next to her and my eyes light up. Maybe she changed her mind about not going. Before I can say anything she coughs into a tissue and I can just make out a faint splatter of red.

"Oh my God, are you okay?"

130

"Aye . . . it's normal. Could you just get me a glass of water?"

That night I dream of the Highlands, of a cottage on a hill, of children playing. And then my dream turns into a nightmare.

20

prudence

April 21, 1629
Edinburgh

IT IS DARK. So dark. But I see a spark of light above me. I push
through the soil, but it is no' dirt that my hand reaches out
and touches. It is solid and familiar. I am buried beneath a
sea of bodies.

I struggle to shift even an inch. Slowly, I move upward,
grabbing on to limbs, pushing off rotting flesh. I wriggle my
way to the top and pull myself from the pile of the dead.
The plague came for me, but it didnae take me. I crawl away
from my would-be grave, grateful for the feel of soil, its
hearty fragrance. But even the robust earth cannae remove
the stench of rot from my nose.

I am weakened from the pox. It came on so very quickly
I didnae have the wits to prepare a tonic that would stop

the sickness. I turn on my back and stare up at the sky. The clear blueness mocks me, the sun harsh on my bruised and blackened skin.

With great care I sit up and stare at the pit that was almost my fate. Bodies are piled one upon another, with no regard for Christian rites or family wishes. Limbs lie askew, tinted dark purple, a telltale sign of the plague. These corpses must be put in the ground as quickly as possible to stop the spread of the terrible pox. A moan drifts up from the pile. A single voice pleading for water, and then a name I cannae make out. A call for someone who will never come. Another plague victim brought and dumped here before properly meeting death.

I spit the dirt from my mouth and slowly, shakily stand. I must go back home and recover my health. I have so much to do.

I spot a plague bearer watching me through his white mask. The nose is hooked, long, like a water bird's. In the snout are stuffed herbs that help to deal with the smell of moving the rotting dead. A few believe the herbs will keep you from getting ill, though anyone who moves pox bodies has already suffered through, and recovered wholly from, the plague. He wears it as protection from the reek of so many rancid dead.

I can tell he is sizing me up under his leather bird mask, determining whether I am a threat.

"I feel," I say, my words just a whisper in the wind. I clear my throat, spit out more dirt, and try to find my voice. I start again, my tone strong and unyielding, "I feel much recovered."

He gives me a curt nod, his eyes boring into my body, and I look down at myself. My clothes have gone awry, my sleeve ripped, exposing too much skin. I catch sight of the mark on my inner arm: an X with a circle through the middle. No one can see this, for I havenae survived the black plague only to be hanged as a witch.

Slowly, with great care, I step around the plague bearer and away from the plague pit and walk toward home. A boy sees me and gasps, running away to his mother's skirts. I look like a beggar, or an ill-used woman, but at least I am alive.

No thanks to her.

I am no' shocked that she let them take me, her love is so fickle as of late. She will regret this betrayal, and all the others accumulated over the years. All the anguish and indignities I have suffered at her hands. She has become something wicked, and I will have my revenge.

21

heather

"EARTH TO HEATHER," my aunt says, waving her hand in front of my face. She says *Earth* like *airth*. "Where's your mind at today, love?"

We're visiting Gram, who is remarkably lucid today. I'm the one who's having trouble focusing. It's the new medicine Dr. Casella prescribed. After taking it for a few days, I've decided to stop. The meds are making me hazy . . . and it's not like they've stopped my weird dreams.

The one last night was so strange, so terrifyingly real. I can still smell the awful stench of rotting bodies. It felt like I was actually there, buried under bodies, clawing my way out of a pit.

It makes me want to focus on the other dream, the one

that wasn't so bad, of the children laughing, playing outside the cottage in the Highlands. That one was more dreamlike, hard to hold on to. For some reason, it's the one that's stuck with me, though. When I woke I knew I had to go there, to see it for myself. To finally find out if my dreams are real or if I'm just insane.

"I was wondering . . . do you think it would be possible for me to visit the cottage in the Highlands?" I get the strange feeling I've been searching for it, even before I had that dream. The reason I felt so compelled to come to Scotland.

"Why? You've never asked before." My aunt takes a sip of tea, and I can feel Gram's eyes on me. I want to say that I just found out about it like, four days ago, but instead I say, "I've just been thinking a lot about our family. I'd like to see where we lived."

"There's no electricity," my aunt warns. "No phone, and forget about Wi-Fi. There is working plumbing, but you'd have to cook your meals in the hearth."

"Well, that sounds fun," I say. "Like camping, but better."

My aunt is still not convinced. "It's a four-hour drive," she tells me. She looks worn, tired. I know she's not up to travel.

"Maybe Fiona could drive. I'll ask Asha to come too. We'll have the ultimate sleepover."

Aunt Abbie considers. "I'll speak with your parents about it." She winces, rubs her stomach. "Those biscuits arenae sitting right. Excuse me." She disappears into the bathroom. She's been throwing up a lot more lately. At least that means that the chemo may be effective after all.

When I look at Gram she's studying me, her deep blue eyes clear. "They speak to me too, you know . . . or at least, they used to."

"Who, Gram?" I ask, clutching my cup a little too tightly, spilling hot tea on myself. I put the cup on the table and grab a napkin.

"The witches."

I pause, drop the napkin onto my lap. "What witches?"

"One had the talent, and one didn't. One accepted the world as it was, and one turned to Blood Magic." She grabs my arm, her grip surprisingly strong. "Do you cut yourself?" she hisses. "Are you hers?"

I try to pull away, but her fingers bite into my skin. "Gram, you're hurting me."

"Mum, what are you doing?" Abbie enters the room and pries Gram's hand from my arm.

"Dinnae let her win," Gram tells me, her voice full of warning.

"I'm sorry, Heather, I dinnae know what's gotten into her. She was doing so well." Aunt Abbie leads Gram to her bed. "I'm going to try to get her to take a nap. Why dinnae you wait in the car."

Outside, I pull my hoodie up against the light rain, my head spinning. Instead of going to the car, I text Asha, asking if she wants to take a walk. When she texts back that she's not busy, I send another text telling my aunt where I'll be. Asha's house isn't far from here, and I need a break from all the weird things that are going on in my life. I need to feel ordinary, even if it's for a few hours. Even if it is a lie.

Gram knows.

"Could we walk at like, a normal pace?" I ask, panting slightly. We're in Holyrood Park, climbing to Arthur's Seat, the highest point in Edinburgh. The rain stopped and the sun is out, making it unreasonably hot for Scotland. We're only about a third of the way up the hill and I'm already tired. Asha is doing this power walking thing that was fine at first, but it's way too much for me now.

Asha glances back at me, slows down. "I know Americans are out of shape, but this is ridiculous."

"Ha-ha." The first part of the trail is steps carved out of the dirt and reinforced with wood. I sit on a patch of grass off to the side so people can pass us. "I'm just not used to . . . well, physical activity. What?" I say off Asha's look. "I watch a lot of movies. It's my thing."

Asha sits next to me. She's not even breathing hard. "I love hill walking. . . . My family went up to the Highlands last year, to the Isle of Skye. There are some really good trails."

"Speaking of the Highlands, do you want to come up to my family's cottage with me?" I ask.

"Your family has a cottage in the Highlands?"

"Apparently. It's old, no electricity or anything. I want to check it out. Maybe we can get Fiona to drive."

"Just don't tell her about the electricity," she says with a laugh. "But it sounds fun to me. When did you want to go?"

"Not sure, maybe this weekend. I need to clear it with my aunt." I look out over the city. "You know, I'm jealous of you guys. You get to live here year-round. You get to hang out whenever you like."

"You could come to university here." Because of her dad's job, Asha already knows she'll be attending Edinburgh University.

I sigh at the thought. "We could even be roommates. Maybe we could all get a flat together. . . ." I trail off when I see Asha's face.

"I can't imagine living with Fiona," she admits. "It's not that I don't love her," she quickly adds. "It's just she's so . . ."

"Fiona," I say with a grin.

She nods. A pair of hikers pass us, a woman and a small child who can't be older than five. Asha gives me a pointed look.

"What?" I ask. "Clearly that kid is some kind of advanced mountain climber. . . ." I sigh. "Just give me one more minute to rest."

"Fine . . . if you fill me in about you and Robby."

"Oh my God, how did I not tell you already? I tried to kiss Robby."

"Wait, what?" She turns to me, brown eyes wide. "What do you mean, tried?"

I tell her what happened, about all the signals I thought I was getting from Robby. About the movie and standing under the overhang. The whole awkward mess.

"I thought he liked me, you know, *liked* me . . . but then he just walked away."

Asha shakes her head. "Heather, you've always been

a bit oblivious when it comes to Robby. He's liked you for years. Anyone can see that."

"Then what's his deal?" I ask.

"Hmmmm . . ." Asha purses her lips.

" 'Hmmmm' what?"

"You can't think of any reason . . . any reason at all why Robby might be acting so hot and cold?"

"No . . . ," I say, and Asha raises her eyebrows at me.

"Robby's older, cuter brother?"

My face drops. "I don't think Alistair is cuter anymore."

"But you did, for years. Do you know how much you used to talk about him? Robby's probably wondering if *you* actually like *him*."

"When we first met up this summer, I did ask him about Alistair . . ." I trail off when Asha gives me another look. "Okay, okay. I'm a jerk. What should I do to let him know I'm interested? Send him flowers? The card can read: *Roses are red, Violets are blue, sorry I was obsessed with your brother for years, but now I really like you.*"

Asha guffaws and another pair of hikers look over at us. One is wearing flip-flops. I stand. "Okay, I'm ready now."

"Just talk to Robby," Asha says. "Or talk to Fiona and I'm sure Robby will hear about it in a matter of moments. You could invite him to the cottage too. If your aunt is there . . ."

"I'm not sure my aunt can come. Is that a problem?" I know it won't be for Fiona. She'll just have to work out her schedule at the café. Asha's parents, on the other hand, might take some convincing.

"Maybe I don't have to tell them she won't be there."

"Asha, you little sneak!"

Her dark skin reddens and she gives me a little shrug. "Well, if you invite Robby, I can invite Duncan—"

"You evil genius!"

"And we can have a little romantic weekend in the Highlands."

"Yes, just the two of you . . . and me . . . and maybe Robby. And Fiona."

She throws up her arms. "Look, let's just make it up this hill first."

"Okay, okay. Let's go. There better be an ice cream shop at the top," I say. Suddenly I feel a shove from behind and my foot catches. I fall facedown in the dirt.

"Are you okay?" Asha rushes to my side. I stand and wipe my hand on my jeans. There's no one around who could have pushed me, and Asha was in front of me. "I just lost my balance, I guess." I let out a shaky laugh. "You know how clumsy I am."

"It looked like you just fell over for no reason." Her mouth drops. "Heather, your jeans . . . you're bleeding."

I look down and find the right side of my jeans stained dark. My carving must have opened up from the exertion.

"Oh, I must have cut myself," I say. I need to get home and change the bandage. "I think I'll head back."

"I'll walk you home," she says, her face full of doubt. "Are you sure you're okay?"

"Yeah, I'm fine. Finish your hike—at least this gets me out of the rest of it." I smile weakly. Asha still looks worried. "And I'll call you later about the trip. It'll be fun."

I turn before she can stop me and head down the hill.

"Heather," my aunt calls, poking her head into my room.

I pause the movie I'm watching on my computer and take out my earbuds.

"Yeah?"

"I wanted to speak with you about Gram." She comes inside and I move over so she can sit next to me on the bed. "I'm sorry if she upset you earlier."

"It's just weird, seeing her freak out like that." I snap my computer shut and push it to the bottom of the bed.

"That's what I wanted to talk with you about. Your doctor, Dr. Casella?"

"Yeah?"

"She contacted me. Your father gave her my number. She wanted me to release your grandmother's medical records since I'm Gram's legal guardian now."

"Did she say anything about me?" I ask.

"No, nothing like that. I just . . . When I emailed her the files, I looked through them first and I found out some things I didnae know."

"Like?"

"When Gram was young—about your age, actually— she . . . well, there's no easy way to say this. She had a mental break. She was committed to a psychiatric ward for a whole year." She shakes her head. "I knew she was always a little strange, but I had no idea she was mentally ill when she was younger."

"What was wrong with her?" I ask.

"According to the records, she used to have these horrible nightmares. They started when she was sixteen."

"You mean night terrors? Like mine?"

Aunt Abbie nods. "Not bad at first, but then . . ." My aunt looks around the room, anything to avoid meeting my eyes.

"Please, tell me," I whisper.

"She started to hear voices. They diagnosed her as schizophrenic and put her on antipsychotics. It didnae help, and she was sent to an institution."

"A real mental institution? Did they hurt her there?"

"Oh, Heather, no. It's not like in those scary movies you watch. They didnae experiment on her or anything. They wanted to help her. It's all in her medical notes."

"So, she just like, got better?" I ask quietly. I can't imagine spending a whole year in a mental hospital. Six weeks at Great Lakes was more than enough for me.

"Aye. Shortly after she turned seventeen, she was released to her parents. She seemed perfectly fine, if a little odd at times. She didnae even have to take medication anymore. I think she just wanted to put that part of her life behind her. I dinnae even know if my father knew about it."

"Poor Gram." I try not to think about what I've been going through lately. At least I don't hear voices. Maybe the night terrors will pass with time, just like Gram's did.

"I didnae tell you all this to make you worry. I wanted to explain to you what I found out. So you'd know what to expect if she gets worse."

"I just wish there was something I could do for her."

God, if Dr. Casella is looking into my family history of mental illness, she must think I'm crazy.

"I also spoke with your parents," my aunt tells me casually. "I mentioned that you wanted to go to the cottage."

"And . . . ?" Despite the awful revelations about my grandmother, I can't help but perk up.

"And they said it was fine as long as I went with you."

My face falls. "It's okay. I know you're not up for it." But it's not okay. I need to get there somehow. My mind whirls with possibilities. I could probably take a bus to the nearest major town, then—

My aunt's voice interrupts my thoughts. "So I told them I would," she says with a grin.

"Wait . . . you're coming?"

She shakes her head. "Heather, I never thought you were a slow one. That's just what I told your parents. I'm letting you girls go without me."

"Thank you, Aunt Abbie!" I lurch across the bed and hug her.

"For lying to your parents?" She laughs. "Not exactly my proudest moment."

"Thank you thank you thank you."

"Calm down," she tells me, and I give her one last squeeze. She's so thin now, I feel like I could break her. "There are conditions, though."

I sit back. "Anything."

"You have to call me as soon as you get there. Your mobile phone may not work, so you'll have to go into town and use one of the landlines."

"Okay. No problem."

"And no alcohol. I know Fiona's a little wild . . . but if she's driving, I want you to make it clear that she will no' be drinking."

"I'll make sure," I promise.

"And lastly, we can never, ever tell your parents I let you go up there without me."

"I thought you were a grown-up and therefore couldn't get in trouble with them," I tease.

"Aye . . . while I cannae be grounded, if anything happened to you, your mother would most certainly kill me."

"I'll never say a word." I mime locking my mouth with a key.

She smiles. "Okay, then. All this emotional sharing is exhausting. I'm going to bed." She stands, plants a kiss on the top of my head. "Good night, Heather."

"Night!" I call after her as I grab my phone from the nightstand.

I call Fiona first and ask her if she wants to come.

"To the Highlands? Why?"

"Because it will be fun. Like an adventure."

"Cannae we have an adventure in Edinburgh? I know where we can get fake IDs made, hit the clubs. . . ."

"As fun as an illegal bender sounds, my aunt lied to my parents so we could go. That's huge. I don't think we'll have another chance."

"So you're lying to your parents . . . and I'm sure Asha's going to have to lie to hers. Not exactly the level of debauchery I hoped for, but I suppose it's better than nothing."

"So you'll come . . . and drive?"

She pauses. "Aye . . . fine."

"You don't have to check with your mom?"

Fiona snorts.

"I mean, your mom doesn't need you to work at the café?" I clarify.

"With the new waiter, I think she can spare me." She pauses, and I can feel her thinking about what she's agreed to. "How old is this cottage, anyway? There better be a working toilet!"

"My aunt assures me that there is indoor plumbing," I say, hoping she won't ask about the electricity.

"Okay, I'll make sure I can borrow the van." There's a slight pause and then she screams, "MUM, CAN I HAVE THE VAN FOR THE WEEKEND FOR A ROAD TRIP TO THE HIGHLANDS WITH ASHA AND HEATHER?" A longer pause. "Heather, she said it's fine."

"Great . . . why can't my mom be that easygoing?"

"Please, I wish my mum was halfway around the world. For a few months, anyway."

I laugh. I can just imagine Fiona completely unsupervised. Edinburgh would not be safe. "Okay, I've got to call Asha."

After I hang up with Fiona I confirm things with Asha. It's all set. I stare at my phone for a long while. Then I pick it up and dial, my heart fluttering in my chest. He answers on the first ring.

"Hey, Robby. How would you like to come with me on a trip to the Highlands?"

22

heather

FIONA'S MOM'S VAN has two seats up front, two in the middle, and a great big seat in the back that can theoretically accommodate three people. The seats fold down for deliveries and up for passengers. So we all fit perfectly, with enough room for all our crap. "Guys, we're only going up there for two nights. What is all this stuff?" I ask, shoving the last of it into the back.

"Ask my mum," Fiona says, adjusting the driver's seat and eyeing us in the rearview mirror. "She packed extra in case we need it."

I sit up front with Fiona. Robby is in one of the middle seats, and Asha and Duncan take the back. Asha giggles, and I refuse to look at what they're doing back there.

Traffic is pretty light for the summer, and soon we're out of the city on the highway up north. I glance back at Robby, only to find him staring at me. I turn around in my seat as far as my belt will allow. "So . . . how's work?" I ask lamely.

"Really good. The tips are great, and the perks just keep coming. You wouldn't happen to want to go to the Highland Games next week? Free tickets . . ."

"That could be fun."

"Can we come?" Asha shouts up. "We can double-date."

"It's not a date," I say, but then look at Robby.

"It could be a date." He grins his crooked grin. "If you want it to be one."

I can feel my face redden. "Or we can make it a group thing," I say. "Then everyone could come without worrying about dates. . . ." I trail off. I catch Fiona watching me sideways. She mouths something that looks like "Coward," and my face warms again.

"As much as I'm loving listening to this super-awkward conversation," Duncan cuts in, "I meant to ask Robby what we're going to do if my mum calls his mum."

"What do you mean?" I ask.

"Well, I told my parents I was at his house, and he told his mom he was at mine," Duncan explains. "Have you never seen an American sitcom? I just know we're going to be found out."

"It's fine," Robby says. "My mum barely ever has her phone. I can guarantee she's not going to call to check up on me."

"So wait," Fiona says. "I'm the only one who didn't lie to

her parents? I feel like I have to do something extra bad just to compete with all of you."

"I'm sure you'll think of something," Asha mutters.

"You didn't tell your mom about this trip?" I ask Robby. Maybe he didn't want her to mention it to my aunt, which would get me in a lot of trouble. Aunt Abbie thinks this is a girls-only excursion.

He lowers his voice. "My mum thinks I shouldnae be spending a lot of time with you."

"Oh." I'm not sure how to take this news, but it feels like a punch in the gut.

He covers quickly. "She just thinks I'll take up too much of your time . . . time you should be spending with your aunt."

"That makes sense," I say, unconvinced.

"It's been hard on my mum. She and Abbie have been best friends forever, and she wants to help her. She's trying to cook up a cancer cure, as if she can figure it out when scientists around the world are stumped."

"Don't tell her," I say, "but Aunt Abbie usually doesn't even take the remedies. I mean, she can barely keep normal food down, much less your mom's gross concoctions."

"Hey, those gross concoctions work," Duncan says. "Mrs. Brodie gave me this face cream that completely got rid of my acne. I mean, one day it was all puss and pimples, and the next, clear as a . . . ." He pauses. "Too much information?"

Robby laughs. "No, Duncan, we all saw your epic acne. We know what a spotty git you used to be."

"No need to be an arse." He reaches up and punches Robby's shoulder. "My point is that her medicines work. Better than the cream I got from the chemist's."

"She fancies herself as an herbal healer," Robby says, rubbing his shoulder.

"If this were the Dark Ages, your mom would be burned as a witch," Asha adds from the backseat.

"She's always been about natural healing and mixing together weird herbal remedies. Remember that shampoo she used to make me and Alistair use?"

"That oregano one?"

"Yeah, I smelled like a bloody pizza." He grins at me, his dark eyes flashing. Then he turns to Asha. "But you know, most witches in Scotland weren't burned. Not alive, anyway."

"They weren't?"

"No. I mean, some were, in the early sixteen hundreds, but halfway through the century they changed tactics. Witches were hanged first, then burned."

"Well, aren't you just brimming with information? Learn that at your job, did you?" Asha teases. "Did they make you read a pamphlet or something?"

"Actually, yes," he admits. "They made all us tour guides read a bunch of history so we'd seem like we knew what we were talking about."

"So why were they hanged and then burned?" I ask.

"Maybe they just wanted to be thorough," Duncan jokes.

"Ever hear of Blood Witches?" I ask, fishing for information.

"Blood Witches?" Fiona says.

"Is that a thing?" Asha asks.

"Sounds like something Heather would like," Fiona calls back over her shoulder to Asha. "She's always watching those scary movies. *Curse of the Blood Witch* sounds like one of those awful films she's always making us watch."

"Ha-ha. You know you love those movies too." I turn to Robby. "I'd never heard of a Blood Witch before this summer."

"Maybe it's a Scottish thing," Duncan ventures.

"Maybe," Robby continues. "Apparently there really were these women, a group of healers, who would mix their blood into their remedies."

"Ewwww," Asha says.

Fiona makes a strange, choked noise.

"Who would do that?" Duncan asks.

"I dinnae know." He shrugs. "Women who thought themselves to be witches. I didnae say *I* did it. I'm just telling you the story. A whole gaggle of witches were caught bleeding into their potions."

"'Gaggle'?" Asha interrupts. "That can't be right."

"Why not? Witches fly on broomsticks. They could be a gaggle," Duncan says.

"Or a flock," Asha offers. "That might work better."

"Coven," I say quietly.

"What, love?" Robby asks.

"A coven. A group of witches is a coven."

Robby looks at me, eyebrows raised.

"I watch a lot of horror movies, remember?"

"Aye, right, of course. So this coven of witches were caught and tried and sentenced to death for consorting with the devil or whatever witches do for fun on a Saturday night. They were supposed to be burned alive, but do you want to know the real freaky part?" he asks, his voice low for effect. "When they went to set them on fire, they would-nae burn."

"They were like, fireproof?" I ask. Gram said that too. A Blood Witch couldn't burn.

"I guess. So after that they started to hang witches."

"So if witches are fireproof, why wouldnae they also be noose-proof?" Duncan asks.

"Seems like a witch could just wave her wand and be sipping sangria in Spain before they even hit the end of the rope," Fiona adds.

"The Blood Witches must have been bloody awful at witching," Duncan says with a grin.

"People died," I say quietly. "Women suffered horrible, torturous deaths." I can almost smell the smoke in my dreams. "Even the ones who weren't burned—they didn't deserve to die."

"I . . . Sorry . . . ," Duncan apologizes. "I didnae think about it like that."

"It did happen four hundred years ago, Heather," Asha says.

"No, you're right." I look over my shoulder and give them a weak smile. "I just meant it was a horrible thing. People who were trying to help, or who were just not well liked, were tormented and killed for no good reason. It's disturbing."

"I don't get it," Fiona says. "Why didn't they burn? How can a human being be fireproof?"

"Are witches human?" Duncan asks. "I thought they were the devil's handmaidens or something."

"It's just a story, mate," Robby tells him. "There is no such thing as a witch."

"He's never met my mother," I mumble, and Fiona laughs. "You know, it's strange," I add. "My gram keeps talking about witches. I mean, she's not all there anymore, but it's making me have some freaky dreams. She mentioned the cottage, and then I had a dream about that, too."

"You must be really suggestible," Asha says.

Robby gives me a wicked look. "So if we talk about something before you go to sleep tonight, do you think you'll dream it?"

"I don't even want to know. . . ."

"You . . . me . . . candlelight . . ."

"In your dreams, Robby," I say, giggling.

"Maybe in yours." He waggles his eyebrows.

"Oh, I love this song." Duncan lurches into the front of the van to turn up the volume.

"Seat belts, please!" Fiona shouts.

Duncan gets halfway back to his seat before pausing next to Robby and pointing out the window. "Ohhh, there's the Scottish Heritage Center. Can we go?" he asks. I look up, not realizing how far out of the city we've gotten. We're making really good time.

"Why?" Fiona asks. "That place is a tourist trap."

"Hey, this is not a fascist regime," Duncan jokes. "If I want to go, I get to go."

"Not when I'm the one driving," Fiona counters. "Unless you jump out as I speed past. Dinnae forget to tuck and roll."

"Please?" He changes tactics and tries begging, giving Fiona puppy-dog eyes. "We'd always go there when I was little. They have a Scottish fudge shop inside and a Highland cow you can pet. It's dead fun."

"What do you guys think?" Fiona asks the rest of us.

"I'd like to pet a Highland cow," Asha says at the same time I respond, "Um, hello, fudge."

Fiona glances at me. "All right. Just a short stop."

We pull into the heritage center parking lot. There's a main building with shopping, and then off to the side is a pen with sheep and cows, a little petting zoo for kids. Highland cows are pretty funny looking. They're big and orange and shaggy.

I get out of the van and stretch my legs.

"So," Asha asks me, "fudge or cow?"

"First, what a strange decision to have to make. Second, have you met me?"

"Fudge it is, then." Asha grabs Duncan's hand and leads the way inside the building. I turn, only to bump into Robby, who is standing inches away.

"Oh, sorry," I say awkwardly.

"No worries." He takes my hand. "You're cold. I'll buy you a cup of tea."

I smile up at him.

"Stop making googly eyes at each other," Fiona shouts from across the parking lot. She's making a beeline for the petting zoo. "And come pet the animals. I'm not going to be the only one smelling like a barnyard."

"Okay, first the petting zoo, then the tea," I say.

"Sounds like a plan." Robby pulls me close, putting his arm around my shoulder.

Fiona kneels next to a sheep, petting its thick curly hair. The sheep reaches out its long tongue and licks Fiona's face, managing to chomp on some of her hair as well. Fiona screeches.

"Um . . . a little help, please," she begs from where she's crouched. "I'd like to get out of this without a bald spot. . . ."

I buy some feed from the keeper, who is laughing at Fiona's antics instead of trying to help her, and distract the sheep with it.

"How did that even happen?" I ask, laughing at her look of disgust as she combs her fingers through her slobbered-on hair.

"That cute-and-cuddly is a bloody act. That thing is a menace."

I look to the sheep, staring at us with big brown eyes. "Yeah, clearly it's evil."

"Let's go get some fudge and tea," Robby says with a wink in my direction.

"Oh, I could murder a cup of tea," Fiona says.

We make our way to the main building, and I put my hand on Fiona's shoulder. "You know, you remind me of my sister."

She looks at me. "Heather, if you had a sister, I think I would know about it."

"I guess I meant you're like a sister to me." A weird feeling suddenly hits me, and I feel the urge to cut. I swallow. "Why don't you go ahead and find Asha and Duncan. I'm gonna head to the restroom."

I hurry to the bathroom, only to find Fiona has trailed after me. "I've got to get this sheep spit out of my hair," she tells me, heading to the sink. She looks at me in the mirror. "You really dinnae look very well."

"Carsick," I call out as I lock myself in one of the stalls and wait for the need to pass. I put down the toilet seat and sit. I'm sweaty, and I wish Fiona would just leave. Eventually she does, but not before asking if I need help.

"I'll be okay in a minute," I say.

I start to count backward from ten. I get to one and start over again. I think of my cuts, of a knife slicing my skin. Why can't I just be normal?

After a while I feel like myself again, if a bit shaky. I go to find the others, hoping they won't ask where I've been, but Fiona's already told them I was ill.

"I get carsick all the time," I lie as Robby hands me a cup of steaming tea.

I'm too drained to feel ashamed.

23

primrose

May 1, 1629
Edinburgh

I SHOULD HAVE healed her. I should have been there for her. Played nursemaid. I should have been here when they came for her, but I wasnae. I was with Jonas. I dinnae dare tell her about him. I wish I could. I wish we were young again, running through the Highlands, the wind in our hair and the grass under our feet. We had no secrets from each other then.

When I came home that night, Prudence was gone. I feared the worst—that she was dead—and I felt inside me a horrific relief alongside my worry and grief. There was no sign of Father. He spends most evenings at the public house down the street. I thought to fetch him, but I knew he would not want me to come, no matter what. All I could do was wait and worry.

Later Prudence stumbled through the door looking like she clawed her way out of a grave and fought death tooth and nail, and then all I felt was a cold shame. She is my sister, and I should not wish her ill. Is my love for this boy stronger than my love for my own flesh and blood? Must they be at odds?

But now I have been by her side for a week, cooped up indoors, cooking and cleaning and being a good sister to her, a good daughter to our father. He didnae even know she had been missing.

I cannae take it. I must see Jonas.

Tonight.

24
heather

THE COTTAGE IS just like I dreamt. It's a little bigger, made of stone, with a modern roof instead of brown thatch, and glass windows, but it's exactly where I dreamt it would be, nestled on a hill. Behind it is a shimmering brook flowing into a small pond set against the green rolling hills of the Highlands. Heather, the plant for which I'm named, dots the landscape, bringing a brilliant purple color to the browns, yellows, and greens.

Robby gets out of the car and stands next to me. "Are you okay?" he asks.

"Yeah. I just . . . I feel like I've been here before."

"When you were little? With your parents?"

"Must be."

Fiona looks around. "Well, here's as good a place to park as any, I suppose."

I eye all the stuff piled high in the back of the van. "Um . . . let's get settled before we bring all this in."

"You have keys, right?" Duncan asks. "For the door?"

"It should be open. There's a man from town who checks on the place once a month. My aunt called him and asked him to leave it unlocked for us."

"She's not worried someone's going to rob it?" Fiona asks.

"Um, look around." I motion at the empty vastness. "There aren't a lot of people out here."

Inside the cottage, the stone hearth looks functional, if a little worn with its hundreds of years of usage. "This must have been part of the original foundation," I say.

A rug lies across the gray stone floor, and a comfy-looking couch and chair face the fireplace. The air inside is cold and smells a little musty, but not unpleasant. There's a side table with old family photos. I pick up one of a girl about my age. Gram. She's smiling, but her eyes don't look happy. No wonder. After what Aunt Abbie told me about Gram hearing voices, the haunted look on her face makes perfect sense. I put the picture down and shiver. My hand misses the table and I drop the frame onto the floor, cracking the glass.

Everyone jumps. "Sorry, guys." I pick up the splintered frame and put it back on the table.

"You scared me half to death," Fiona says. "I nearly wet myself." That gets a giggle from the boys and a smile from Asha.

"Yeah, this place certainly has atmosphere," Asha says.

"If by 'atmosphere' you mean it's creepy, I totally agree," Fiona says.

"A whole family lived in this one room?" Duncan asks.

"And the livestock in the winter," Robby adds, "so they could keep warm." Asha looks at him, eyebrows raised. "What? I know what I'm talking about. I read a pamphlet."

I go through a door to the right and there's a small bedroom with a bathroom, "recent" updates that were made in the past century. The sink and tub are old-fashioned but have held up well, and the toilet is more modern. Gram must have replaced that at some point.

"I call the toilet!" Fiona rushes through and slams the door. "I still have sheep drool in my hair!"

Duncan puts his stuff in the bedroom and Asha follows, giving me a shy smile.

"That's sorted, then," Robby whispers.

"I guess the rest of us can all sleep in the living area like one big happy family," I say. "Did anyone besides me bring a sleeping bag?"

"Aye, my mum made me pack three," Fiona says, rejoining us. "What?" she asks as I give her a blank stare. "She's been busy with the café lately, but we used to go camping all the time. I bloody hated it, but I learned a few things."

I shiver again. It seems colder inside than outside, if that's at all possible. "Let's get a fire started and have some tea."

"I saw some chopped-up wood outside," Robby says. "The caretaker must have left it."

Once Robby brings the wood inside, he and Duncan try to build a fire.

"Let the big strong men handle this," Duncan says in a deep, macho voice.

Asha shakes her head. "I'd feel better if either of you big strong men weren't hopeless city boys."

"Sorry, but that's not going to work," Fiona tells them. "The wood is too wet. Even if it lights, it will make the room all smoky. I brought dry wood," she tells us. "Just in case."

"Bloody hell, *that's* why your bags are so heavy," Robby says.

"Well, I feel useless," Duncan says with a sheepish grin.

Asha hugs him. "You're not useless. You have other talents."

While the boys and Fiona get the fire going, Asha and I unload the van. My cell phone has zero bars, so Fiona agrees to drive me back into town so I can call my aunt. Asha asks to come too.

It's a relief to be away from the boys, if even for just a moment. We stop at the little village's one tiny shop, which seems to be the town grocery store, liquor store, and hardware store. It has the most random assortment of wares. "Look," Fiona says. "You can buy whisky *and* some yarn to knit a wooly sweater."

"Now, that's convenience," Asha says.

"Do you have a phone?" I ask the woman behind the counter, who eyes me warily.

She looks me up and down. "There's a pay phone at the side of the store." A pay phone? Really?

"I didn't know those still existed," I say.

Under her breath the woman mutters, "City folk."

"Can I have some change?" I ask, holding out a fiver.

She gives me a look. "I'll no' open the register unless you buy something."

"Okay . . ." I look around. "Hey, guys, maybe it would be fun to make s'mores."

"What's that?" Asha asks.

"You've never had s'mores?" I say, widening my eyes. Unfortunately the shop doesn't have graham crackers, but I decide Scottish shortbread will be a good substitute. Miraculously, Asha finds some marshmallows and chocolate, and we bring our haul up to the counter.

The woman stares at Fiona. "I heard that Iain MacNair's daughter was coming with her friends."

"Yeah, that would be me," I say.

"But you're American."

"I sure am. . . ." She stares at me, trying to figure out if I'm lying, and I don't know what else to say. "Can I get some change now?"

She rings up our food on an ancient register, typing the price in and pulling a lever on the side for each item. She's taking her sweet time but manages to stop staring at me long enough to notice Asha. "And where are you from, dearie?"

"Edinburgh," she says.

"No, I mean *originally*." She takes forever to bag up the food and hand me my change.

"Edinburgh," Asha repeats, a hint of confusion in her voice. Then understanding dawns. "But . . . my family came from India ages ago."

"Oh, India, right. It's so nice that they made it here. I hear India is just dreadful."

"Thanks," I say, heading out of the store and dragging Asha after me before the woman can insult her further. We find the pay phone around the side of the building, and I take a moment to marvel at it. This whole place feels like it's stuck in the past.

Once Asha and I make our check-in calls and get in the van, Fiona grins at us.

"What?" I say.

She holds up a bottle of booze and shakes it. Drambuie. "Where did you get . . . You did *not* just steal that?"

"What?" she says, her voice sweetly innocent. "I told you I'd have to do something bad to outdo you two lying about the boys coming with us."

I look back at Asha. "And you're okay with this?"

She shrugs. "I think I can condone Fiona stealing from a horrible old racist lady."

"She was kind of racist, wasn't she?" I do a false Scottish accent in falsetto. " 'Oh, you're from America? I'm so sorry for you. I hear it's just horrible there. And dinnae get me started on India. . . .' "

Fiona giggles and Asha guffaws.

"Well, are you going to report me to the local authorities?" Fiona asks.

"They'd probably just lock me up for being American and having a bad influence on you. You'd get away free and clear."

Fiona grins and starts the car. I was so excited to come to the Highlands, but now I just have a bad feeling, like my skin is too small for my body. I rub my arms.

"You okay, Heather?" Asha asks.

"Fine, just . . ." I look out into the misty woods. "This place just makes me feel strange. It has a lot of family history."

"Yeah, I feel the same way when I visit India. I don't really belong there, but it's kind of familiar. . . ."

Asha talks about India, and I try to keep myself from shivering. The shadows in the woods are definitely moving, and not in a trees-in-the-wind kind of way.

Don't be paranoid, I tell myself. I make myself breathe and count backward from ten. By the time I get to five, I feel better and join in the conversation, which has moved on to Asha's internship, but my eyes stay on the woods, looking for more in the shadows.

"Who wants more sc'mores? That's Scottish for s'mores," I say, waving my fork.

"I don't care what you call them, they're delicious," Fiona says.

We're gathered around the fire, happily eating s'mores. With no metal skewers, it's a little hard to pull off s'mores, but I'm doing my best.

"I'll have another one," Robby says. I'm using a fork to torch the marshmallows in the fire. Not ideal. I'm careful to let the flames just lick the marshmallow, and not to actually heat the metal of the fork. I don't want to get burned. I think about all the lore I've been hearing lately about Blood Witches. I reach my hand farther into the fire. The wood pops and an ember lands on my hand.

"Ow, crap!" I drop the fork into the fire, the marshmallow quickly burning into a charred lump.

"Heather, are you okay?" Robby asks.

"Yeah, just a little burn. I guess I'm not a Blood Witch after all."

"Did you actually think you were?" he asks with a grin. "You really are suggestible."

Fiona hops up. "I brought burn salve. . . . Robby's mum actually made it for my mum to use in the kitchen."

"Wow, how prepared are you?" I say. She gets the salve and puts it on my hand. "Thanks. Well, I'm done with being the s'mores bitch. Let's watch a movie."

I set up my computer and place it on the side table so everyone can see, then take a seat on the floor between Robby and Fiona. We pushed back the couch and set up the sleeping bags to make one big comfy bed. Fiona pulls out the bottle she took from the town store. She takes a sip and passes it to me.

"Um, no thanks."

"Come on, it's good. It tastes like sweet whisky."

"That sounds disgusting." I sniff it and it doesn't smell half bad. I take a small sip. It burns on the way down but leaves a sugary taste in my mouth.

"Want some?" I ask Robby.

"Maybe just a wee dram." He takes a sip. Both Asha and Duncan decline, so Fiona takes another drink.

We pass the bottle back and forth, and soon I'm feeling tired. I close my eyes as I snuggle into my sleeping bag. It's a strange exhaustion, because I'm also exhilarated at being so close to Robby, at sneaking the boys up here and coming without my aunt.

I drink more of the alcohol than I should.

The air in the cottage feels heavier somehow.

And cold.

25

pruдence

May 1, 1629
Eдinburgh

ON THIS DARK, starless night I walk the streets of Edinburgh, my footsteps echoing eerily on the stone. I dinnae mind the cold, nor the rain, nor the smell of the city, but it is late and I would rather be home in bed. I am up because of Primrose. I awoke to her sneaking out the window. I wanted to follow her, needed to follow her. She is up to mischief; of that there is no doubt.

I thought her oblivious to the world, lost in her own thoughts, but in front of me Primrose suddenly pauses. I halt as well. I feel like a wolf stalking its prey. She tilts her head and listens, and I hold my breath. I dinnae want her to see me. Whatever wickedness she intends, I plan to catch her in the act.

She rounds a corner and I slowly follow her, peeking my head around the stone wall. A man nearly bumps into me, and I can smell his sour breath, reeking of whisky. He leers at me, but my look dissuades him and he stumbles on his way.

I spot her again, farther up the road, and hurry to catch up. I needn't have bothered, since she has arrived at her destination, a run-down doorway where a man barely older than a boy eagerly awaits.

"Jonas," she breathes, falling into him. He reaches out to her and holds her close, his mouth hungrily closing on hers. I cannot help the sharp gasp that escapes my lips. Her kissing a boy on the street for all to see, no better than a common whore.

The boy clenches her arm, his want apparent, and an old familiar feeling trills inside me. Envy. The green-eyed monster rears its ugly head, and it is all I can do not to confront her now. Father will have her whipped for this, for meeting a boy in the middle of the night, for acting immodestly. She's always been his favorite, has always had him fooled, but now he will see her as she is: deceitful and conniving. He will see her for her true self.

The clouds part, and the moon's light beams down on the street. Primrose turns, as if suddenly ashamed to be doing things in the light that ought to be hidden in shadow. I see her perfectly, from her long golden hair to the gentle curve of her chin to the slight bump on her otherwise perfect nose. Her face is etched into my memory. I want nothing more than for her look of joy to turn to one of pain. And I promise it will; by heaven and hell, it will.

I hurry home. The house is dark. Father is no doubt at the pub. I quickly gather my ingredients.

That boy is whom she has forsaken me for? Then I will have him.

I crush the herbs with a pestle, then place them in a satchel. I take a knife and slice my finger, dripping blood onto the bundle.

She returns as I leave, and I ignore her questioning look. I return to their meeting spot, his home, and knock on the door. He opens it and greets me with a ready smile.

"I thought you had to hurry home to your da."

I set my face into a wicked smile. "I was halfway there when I remembered I had made something for you."

I push past him into his one-room hovel. The kettle is already boiling, and I find a cup in the satchel I secreted in my pocket. I put the mixture in and pour the water over it.

"Drink this," I tell him. He blows on it to cool it, and sips it.

"You want me," I say.

"Of course . . ." He takes another gulp of his drink. "Primrose . . ."

I shake my head and he stops, drops his cup. "You are the sister. Prudence."

I nod and step closer. "You want me."

"I . . ." He looks confused. "I love Primrose."

I step closer still, until there is no room between us. "You may love her, but you want me." The potion has done its job, creating a lust so great he has no choice but to sate it with me, especially when I pour into it all my intent, all my suggestion.

I take from Primrose all that I can.

170

26
heather

WHEN I WAKE up the next morning, my mouth feels weird, dry and sticky, so I go to the bathroom and drink some water from the tap. Everyone is sleeping in the living room, including Asha and Duncan, despite having claimed the bedroom for themselves. Robby is nowhere to be found.

I look around the room, my gaze settling on the flame low in the fireplace. These dreams I have . . . why is it that when I was Edinburgh I dreamt about the Highlands, and now that I'm in the Highlands I'm dreaming about Edinburgh? What does it all mean?

I place more wood on the fire and touch the warm stone around the mantel, my hand trailing along the seams. I find what I'm looking for, a little nook, and a voice whispers in my head, *You cannae be sure unless you look.*

I tug at the stone and nothing happens. I let out a little laugh and Asha asks groggily, "Heather, what are you doing?"

I turn with a start. "Nothing. I just thought there was something here."

She comes up behind me, examines the hearth. "It looks like that stone is loose."

I pull at it harder and it gives way all at once, causing me to fall back onto my butt. I laugh and Asha grins, then whispers, "Shhh, the others are sleeping."

"More like trying to sleep," Fiona whispers loudly. She comes over to us, blanket wrapped around her shoulders, her red curly hair crazy-wild. "Why are you pulling apart your cottage?"

I look into the hole I created by removing the hearthstone. "There's something hidden in here."

I move forward, and Asha warns, "You probably don't want to put your hand in there. You'll cut yourself."

I ignore her and reach into the hole. My fingers brush against cloth and I grasp a bundle, pulling it from its hiding spot.

"What is that?" Fiona asks.

"I . . . I don't know." I unwrap the cloth carefully, and dried herbs flutter to the floor as I see what I hold in my hands. A book, ancient and worn, but not as damaged as it should be after centuries buried under a hearth. I touch the leather cover. It's the grimoire. The one from my dream.

"Heather, that looks really old," Asha says. "Maybe you

shouldn't handle it. I think you need special gloves or something."

I can't help it; I have to see what's inside. I open the book, turn each page. The front pages are the oldest, the ink faded, the words written in a language I don't understand. But as I turn the pages and the handwriting changes, and changes again, the words become legible, written in English: names of plants and herbs. Generations of knowledge are collected here.

"I think . . . I think this is a healer's book," I say.

"You mean one of your ancestors hid it there?" Fiona asks.

"Maybe."

Asha shakes her head. "You should bring it back and show your aunt. I'm sure she can get someone at the university to look at it. Or I can give it to my father and—"

"You're not going to tell me it belongs in a museum, are you?"

"It might. . . . Wait . . . is that a movie reference?"

"Yeah, but don't worry. I'll show it to my aunt." I retrieve the cloth from the floor and rewrap the book. Then I wrap it in one of my sweaters and place it in my backpack.

I feel like I have to be by myself to process what just happened. "I . . . I need to get some air," I tell them.

Asha nods. "I'll start breakfast."

"Aye. You do that. And I need to get some more sleep." Fiona goes back to her place, cuddles up in her blanket.

I put on a sweater, slip on my shoes, and sneak out, careful not to wake anyone else.

I stand just outside the door, staring into the wooded area.

There's always a point in scary movies when the main character is confronted with some strange evidence and they have to decide to believe the impossible or continue on with their eyes closed to the truth. Usually, the ones who refuse to believe in ghosts/aliens/zombies are the ones who die horrible, gruesome deaths.

So either I (a) believe I'm crazy or (b) start to believe in magic, in the ability to see into the past. Even if I choose (b), that still makes me feel like I'm completely raving crazy. The thing is that even if I think about it logically, the only thing that makes sense is (b).

My dreams can be explained away, but not this. Not finding the grimoire exactly where I dreamt it would be.

I walk around the side of the cottage, toward the hills, and spot Robby down by the pond. He hears me approach and turns around.

"I was just looking out over the loch." Mist hovers just above the water's surface, pouring in from the hills. "This place . . . it's . . ."

"Bewitching," I say.

He turns to me, inches closer. I look into his dark eyes as he reaches up to my face. I think he's going to fix my hair, like he's done before, but his hand lingers on my cheek.

"Heather . . ."

"Yes?" His face is so close to mine. He bends down slightly; his lips brush mine softly. I'm frozen in the moment, and he pushes forward, his lips now greedily kissing mine. His hand gently caressing my cheek. I reach up and place my hand on his neck, and hungrily kiss him back.

I didn't know a kiss could be like this, all-consuming. A voice at the back of my mind whispers, *You wicked girl. What have you done?*

The rest of the day we spend walking the hills and hiking through the woods. Asha knows a lot of different plants and names each one. Then Asha and Duncan sneak off for a while, and Fiona decides to remain in the cottage, draining the last of my computer battery.

Robby holds my hand, but it's different from before. Where his skin touches mine, I feel tingly. I can't stop looking at him. How have I never noticed how cute he is? How did I spend all those years crushing on his older brother?

That night we have a bonfire. I sit far from it, the flames unsettling. When Robby beckons me closer, patting the sleeping bag he brought out to sit on, I suck it up and ignore the way the fire makes me feel, like at any moment I could spontaneously combust.

I distract myself by telling ghost stories to the group. First I tell one about the Baobhan sith, which is a kind of sexy Scottish vampire that lures men to their deaths so it can drink their blood. After that I tell the story of my ancestor who haunts the cottage. It's complete rubbish, and I make the whole thing up, but it must be pretty convincing because Asha hides her head in her hoodie and refuses to come out until Duncan threatens to tickle her.

Then Robby decides to tell a family-friendly Scottish folktale . . . about a man who got drunk and fell asleep in the woods. Three girls find him and try to wake him but can't, he's so sound asleep.

"So one of the lassies takes a blue ribbon out of her hair, lifts up his kilt and . . ."

"Robby, that's not exactly family friendly," I say.

He grins. "Okay, well, she ties the ribbon somewhere any man would immediately notice. When he wakes, he spots the ribbon and says, 'I dinnae know where you've been, laddie, but you've won first prize!'"

Duncan guffaws and Fiona says it would have been funny, but she's heard it a million times, and Asha says, "I don't get it." Then Duncan explains and she giggles.

"Robby . . . ," I whisper.

"Aye, love?"

"Should we maybe say something to them . . . about us?" I ask, glad it's dark and he can't see my face redden.

"Aye." He stands, pulling me up to my feet. "I know just how to tell them." He sweeps me in his arms and lowers me like we're in some dance . . . or an old black-and-white film. He kisses me, and for a moment I forget where we are and who we're with. Robby is all there is.

Then I hear Fiona whoop and Duncan say, "It's about bloody time." Robby places me back upright and I sit, flustered and embarrassed.

After an awkward pause I desperately want the focus to be on anything else, so I say, "Oh, Robby, I forgot to tell you, but I found a book today. It was hidden in the hearth." I'm a little too close to the fire. The heat from the flames licks my skin. I shiver and scoot back.

"It looks old," Asha says. "She's going to bring it to the university to have it examined."

"Heather thinks it's a witch's book," Fiona adds.

"I don't. I was just thinking about how magical this place is. I'm open to, I guess, the idea of otherworldly possibilities."

" 'Otherworldly possibilities'?" Duncan asks.

"Well, what do *you* guys think of magic? Do you think maybe those women . . . the Blood Witches . . . really could heal?"

"Sure, with the right mixture of herbs, why not?" Robby says.

"I think she means actual magic," Asha clarifies. She's right. I want someone to say it, someone to agree that magic can be real. That I'm not crazy.

"Tell me you dinnae believe in that," Duncan says. "Asha, I thought you were too smart for that."

"No need to be condescending," Asha tells him. "My awa, my dad's mom, was born in India. They believe in all kinds of stuff there. I mean, my grandfather came to this country because a swami had a dream that they would be prosperous here."

"Really?" I ask. "Like, a prophetic dream?"

"That's what my grandfather thought. It's funny, because the swami said they would raise a family here, but my grandparents' children were all grown up by then. And after they got here, my awa got pregnant with my dad. He was their late-life surprise. Whenever my dad gets too uptight or worried about things, they remind him that he was the result of some mystic man's dream."

"And what do you think?" I ask Duncan.

"I think I can dream that it's going to rain, and maybe it will, but just because it does doesnae mean I'm a prophet. There are all kinds of explanations for stuff like that."

"Aye," Robby says. "Like a big fat coincidence."

"I'm glad your grandfather came here because someone had a dream," I tell Asha. "Or we would have never met."

"Well, you already know my mom believes in all that spiritual healing nonsense," Robby says. "You've all been to the shop, seen the hippieness."

"Maybe it's not nonsense," Fiona says. "Seventeen years ago my mum wanted to have a baby. So she went to Robby's mum for a love potion."

"What?" Robby asks. "How have I never heard about this before?"

"Because it's completely mental." She grins. She holds up the near-empty bottle of whisky. She must have stolen more than just the Drambuie from the shop. "And I wasnae drunk then."

"Well, get on with it," Duncan says. "Tell us the story."

"So, my mum used the love potion on my da, got him to spend a few nights with her, and then when she got pregnant, released him from all responsibility."

"How romantic," Asha says.

"That's not the point," Fiona tells her. "My mom wanted a baby, and she used magic to get me . . . at least, that's what she says."

"And you believe this?" Duncan asks.

Fiona grins. "Naw. The real love potion was a few glasses of Scotch and some risqué lingerie."

178

"And what about you, Heather?" Asha asks. "Do you think there are things like love potions and prophetic dreams?"

"I dreamt this cottage," I say quietly. "I dreamt that the book would be exactly where I found it."

No, says a voice at the back of my head. *Dinnae tell them.*

I should have known what would happen. That they'd look at me exactly as they are now, faces full of disbelief.

"Guys, I'm just joking," I say with a forced laugh.

Asha's face brightens. "Oh, you really had me going there. You sounded so serious."

Robby pulls me to him and we cuddle up by the fire. I look at the cottage, light from the fire dancing off the stone walls. The side windows look like two dark eyes staring at me. Was a woman really murdered in there? I dreamt that, too.

"Let's sleep out here tonight," he says, wrapping the sleeping bag around us.

"Okay," I immediately agree, snuggling into his warm arms. It takes me a long while, but finally I fall asleep under the clear, starry sky.

27

primrose

May 20, 1629
Edinburgh

I FORGAVE HIM; of course I did. How could I no'? He is no' to blame—her dark magic is. I explained it all, afraid that he would no longer love me because of what my family—what I—can do, but he only pulled me tighter. He said he was devoted to me no matter what comes and that he was sorry for his betrayal.

But it was her betrayal.

And now she tells me that she is carrying his child, though it has been hardly a month since she seduced him. In my anger, I threatened to tell Father about it, but she knows I wouldnae. She holds Jonas over me like a guillotine. We are at a stalemate.

I offered to help keep her pregnancy a secret, to take the

child with me when I leave with Jonas. I told her that we will raise it as our own and she need not be stained in the eyes of Father or the Church.

She laughed in my face. She told me that she will take care of the child herself, one way or another. I shudder to think what she means.

Perhaps it is better. I dinnae think that I could hate a child, especially one who is part Jonas, but I dinnae need a constant reminder of what Prudence has done to me. And this means that Jonas and I will no' have to wait nine months to leave. We can go ahead as planned. This time next month I shall be back in the Highlands, a married woman, and one day a mother myself.

And I will never see Prudence again.

28
heather

LEAVING THE HIGHLANDS makes me feel sad. Like I've lost something I can't quite explain. I'm quiet on the drive back, and between Fiona and Duncan arguing about music and Robby asking if we should stop at the Scottish Heritage Center again to visit Fiona's boyfriend, the sheep, it's pretty easy for me to keep to my thoughts. As crazy as it sounds, I've accepted that my dreams are a window onto the past.

"Where's your mind today, Heather?" Robby asks. We're back in Edinburgh. Nearly to my street. "We're okay . . . aren't we?"

I smile. "Of course we are. I'm just tired."

"I'm knackered from all this driving," Fiona says. "I'm going to sleep for a week."

I say my good-byes as we pull in front of my aunt's house. I still feel awkward about me and Robby liking each other, but he doesn't seem to have any problem with it. He steps out of the van and leans into me. His kiss leaves me breathless.

"I had fun," he says. "I hope we have more fun soon."

"We will," I say with a flushed smile. He squeezes me again and I float through the door and up the stairs. When I get to my aunt's flat, though, I come crashing back to earth. My aunt sits at the kitchen table and looks so small, so frail. I wish there were something I could do to help her.

I insist she rest in bed while I tell her about the weekend, leaving out the fact that Robby and Duncan were there. After she falls asleep, I go to my room and take out my computer, remembering that Fiona drained the battery, and plug it in to charge. I also remove my clothes from my bag, and the bandages I'm sure to always have on hand. All that's left is the book wrapped in cloth.

I carefully lift the grimoire and place it on the bed. The brown leather cover is worn with age. There's a mark on it that I didn't notice before. At first I think it's a flaw in the leather, but it was made on purpose. I take out a piece of paper and lay it on top of the cover, then carefully shade with my pencil. I hold the paper up to the light. It's slight, but it's there: a large Trinity knot.

I push the paper aside and open the book, touching each page with care. Asha is right, I probably should be wearing special gloves or something, but though the pages look old, they don't feel fragile like ancient paper should.

The first pages are written mostly in Scots Gaelic. In the

middle of the book, Gaelic and English words are mixed together. The last pages are completely in English, though an archaic form.

I continue to flip through the book, my mind half on Robby, half on what the grimoire means. Women in my families were witches. . . . Does that mean I'm a witch too? I stop on a page with a spell that looks simple enough, but I don't know where to get ingredients like fresh lavender. I doubt they have it at the corner shop. Maybe an organic market? Fiona would know.

I call her. "Are you home now?" I can hear the din of the café in the background.

"Aye. And back to work," she says. "I wanted to sleep, but my mum said we need the extra hands. The new waiter's holding his own, though."

"The sexy waiter with the dreamy eyes?" I ask.

"That's the one."

I pause. "Does your mom still go to that farmers' market on Tuesday afternoons?"

"Aye, she always drags me along so I can learn the business. As if I care."

"Well, if I give you a list of things, can you get them for me?"

"Like what?" I can hear the curiosity in her voice.

"Herbs, mostly . . . and some other things."

"Why on earth would you want herbs?" Then she groans. "Oh my God. It's that book, isn't it?" she asks. "You're going to try and do a spell." Fiona pretends to be a bubblehead, but she's pretty sharp.

"Maybe . . ."

"Is there a love potion in there?" she asks excitedly.

"I don't know. I'll have to look."

"Well, I'll get the stuff if you make up a love potion for me."

"Yeah, okay," I say. "Um . . . do you actually think it will work?"

"I don't care. I want to give it a try. Text me the ingredients and I'll get everything. Deal?"

"Deal."

"Okay, gotta go. Got a ton of fat tourists to feed. See you soon."

I hang up the phone and scour the book, quickly turning each page. I know I'm handling it a bit too roughly when I get a nasty paper cut and drip blood onto the leather, leaving a dark brown stain. I take a deep breath. This thing is hundreds of years old and I'm not being very careful with it. I get a bandage for my finger, and when I return I gingerly turn the pages, searching for Fiona's love potion.

There's something about "encouraging amorous feelings," which is exactly what Fiona wants. I text her a list of ingredients, along with ingredients for a healing salve. Will these potions work? I need to know.

I put the grimoire away in one of the drawers of my nightstand and lie back on my bed, my head fuzzy. I suddenly feel warm, like I did when I drank all that Drambuie. My face and arms are flushed and I'm a bit dizzy. I close my eyes and try to sleep.

29

prudence

June 5, 1629
Edinburgh

MY PLAN HAS backfired. I thought her will would be broken, her hope torn from her breast, leaving her in disarray, but she forgave him. She is as determined as ever to elope, to leave me forever. I cannae let her. I willnae let her have her happily-ever-after.

She thinks I may be lying about the child who grows within me, but I am no'. Am I to be stuck with the stigma of a baby out of wedlock while she runs away to find her happiness? I hate her optimism. I hate her.

I whisper in our father's ear my doubts about her, tell him he knows what our mother was, what Primrose is, but he refuses to hear. He has grown weak in his old age. A whisky-soaked shell of the terrible man he once was.

So instead, after church, I speak with the bishop. He is very interested to learn what I know. Very interested indeed.

Primrose will soon be gone, but no' in the way that she thinks.

30
heather

Asha shows up the next morning, bright and early. She lets herself into my room and opens the blinds. I groan and put the covers over my head.

"Hey, on my way to have a jog with the running club, but I wanted to stop by and drop something off first."

I grudgingly sit up. Sure enough, she's in running shorts and a tank top. "It's seven-thirty in the morning. Tell me you brought coffee."

"Actually, I brought you a book," she tells me, handing it over. It's thick and smells like mothballs.

"Great. Thanks." I toss it at the foot of the bed. "You do know it's summer, right?"

She rolls her eyes. "I was speaking to my dad about the book *you* found. . . . Where is it, by the way?"

"In my side-table drawer."

"Heather, it should probably be looked at by someone at the university. Maybe it could be put on display."

"Okay. And how does that relate to *this* book?" I ask. Flopping toward the foot of the bed, I grab the musty thing and hold it up.

"Well, me talking to my dad about your book led to a conversation about Blood Witches," she says.

"As all things seem to do these days."

"And," she continues, "he promised to find more about them for me, so he pulled strings with his librarian friends in the history department, and ta-da!"

"Wait." I sit up. "This whole book is about Blood Witches?"

"No, unfortunately . . . but there are a few paragraphs on them." She opens the book to a bookmarked page and hands it to me.

I sleepily scan the words. "Um, Asha," I say, suddenly wide-awake. "This mentions my family!"

"Yeah, I know. You're welcome." She heads out the door and calls over her shoulder, "Text me later if you want to hang out."

And I read.

The witch trials were a dark time for Scotland, an era that stretched centuries. Finger-pointing was easy, and the burden of proof was trivial at best. Signs of witchcraft included the presence of a mole or scar, talking to oneself, or having too many cats.

One family was especially plagued by accusations of witchcraft. The MacNair family had a record twenty-three women punished for practicing dark arts over a two-and-a-half-century period. Starting with Primrose MacNair, who was burned at the stake, and ending with Hester MacNair, who was accused of being a Blood Witch and hanged, then burned, her body thrown in the loch.

Although the history of Blood Magic is sketchy, it was believed to be a more insidious form of witchcraft, one that bled the soul of the practitioner.

I take a shaky breath and close the book. It's real. It's all real. I knew when I found the grimoire that my dreams were more than dreams, but this . . .

Primrose was a real person. And so was Prudence.

I close the book and throw it on my bed. The day is bright, and I open the window and stare out at the Meadows. People are laughing, kids are playing. How could such a beautiful world hide such darkness?

31

primrose

June 8, 1629
Edinburgh

I PLUNGE INTO the loch, the cold making me release the breath I had hoped to hold. I struggle against my bonds, but to no avail. My hands are tied behind me, my feet bound painfully to my wrists. This is it. I am going to die.

No, the water willnae kill me. But when they see that I havenae drowned, when they find me unharmed, I am doomed.

I have never been so alone.

I hold out as long as I dare, but my body forces me to inhale the icy water. If I were a normal girl, this would be the end. I would be dead. Drowned. Proven righteous. But I am no' normal, and I draw breath from the water . . . no' as easily as if it were air, but it will sustain me as long as I am submerged.

If I sink to the bottom, will they leave me down here, trapped forever in the cold darkness—unable to escape my binds—until I starve or freeze to death? I wish they could understand: I have no evil powers, nothing that would harm them. I only wish to help, to heal. I am no' the devil's hand-maiden, and I am no' immortal; far from it. I just cannae meet my death at water's hands. No' when there is so much life in it from which to draw.

My body refuses to sink, and I bob to the surface, my head breaking the water, the air slapping my face. My salva-tion is also my doom. I feel the bite of metal on my skin as I am hooked by the binds at my arms and pulled from the loch. I cough water onto the earth and greedily suck air into my lungs, which are much relieved to breathe lightly again.

My shoulders throb from my extraction from the water. But that is the least of my concerns. I hear the murmurs of the spectators. "She didnae drown. She is a witch."

I can no longer feel my limbs, but still the cold pierces my core like a sword through my heart. All I crave is warmth. Men surround me, floating in and out of my vision. Dressed in kilts, they are members of the brute squad employed by the Church to test witches.

"Please," I whisper. "Please help me."

"Even now, she calls out to the devil!" someone yells.

"You willnae find Satan here, evil wench."

Someone kicks my back, and a newfound pain shoots down my spine. Another swift kick lands on my head, and I welcome the blackness that follows. Even if it be death.

32

ḫeatḫer

I JOLT FORWARD, hitting my head on the window. I'm breathing hard, and I count backward from ten, forcing myself to open my eyes when I reach one. My breath has left a mist on the glass, and I back away, focusing on the opaque circle.

Dreams are one thing . . . but this was a vision. Dr. Casella would call it a hallucination. Not that I would tell her. They'd lock me up and throw away the key.

I stand and go to the mirror, lifting my arm and pulling up my sleeve, exposing the spiral I have etched into my skin.

There's no one I can tell. My aunt has enough to deal with. So do my parents. I need to calm down.

I am completely on my own.

"So we're making a potion, right?" Fiona asks, dumping all the ingredients onto the kitchen table. "Shouldnae we have a boiling cauldron or something?"

"I don't think that's how it actually works," I say. "We need to mix the herbs up and put them in some cloth, then pour boiling water over it. Then you give it to the boy to drink. And voilà!"

She wrinkles her nose. "So basically, I make him a cup of tea?"

"Hey, you're the one who wanted a love potion."

"I brought this, too." She hands over a bowl and pestle. "It's my mum's."

We gather the love herbs: lavender, yarrow, fennel, and basil, and a few more things I had to look up on the Internet to identify. We chop them up in the food processor, and then I smush them all together and put them in a tea bag that I emptied of tea.

"That should do it," I tell Fiona doubtfully.

"Wait!" She takes one of the steak knives from the counter and gives her finger a poke. A drop of blood falls to the table. She lets the next drop hit the tea bag, then wraps her finger in a paper towel.

"What. The. Hell?" I ask.

"It needs blood to work," she tells me with a wicked grin.

"You're going to let this boy drink your blood?" I ask. "That is beyond gross."

"It's just a drop. It's what my mum did. He won't even know it."

"And you don't see a problem with that?"

"I dinnae have to stand here and have you judge me," she says in an exaggerated huff. She grabs the tea bag and puts it in her purse. "I'll do what I bloody well please with my bodily fluids."

"All right, calm down." I look at the clock. "You have to get to the café, don't you?"

"Yeah, I'll let you know how this works," she tells me with a wink.

After she leaves, I try the healing herbs. I put them on my own scars and wait twenty minutes to wash them off. All that happens is I smell like an herb garden.

When my aunt gets home she raises an eyebrow at the mess in the kitchen.

"Dinner gone wrong?" she asks.

"Slightly."

"I'll order a pizza, then, shall I?"

I clean while we wait for the pizza, and we spend the rest of the night watching TV. I'm about to go to bed when I get a call from Fiona.

"Let me guess," I answer. "The love potion worked and now you're engaged?"

"Not quite, but I do have a beautiful Spanish boy in my bed," she whispers excitedly.

"Fiona! What happened?"

"After work I made him the tea and he asked if I wanted to get a drink and I told him that I had a bottle in my room and we started snogging and the rest is X-rated. It was the love potion."

"Sure, and it has nothing to do with the fact that you're tall and gorgeous and outgoing." I'm surprised it took her this long to snag the waiter.

"No, he didn't look at me twice till I gave him that tea. Look, I gotta go. He's waking up."

I shake my head. All Fiona needed was a reason to talk to him; the potion was her excuse. Still . . .

I go to the kitchen and remake the healing mixture. My aunt's asleep, so I chop everything by hand and smush it with the pestle. At the last moment I take the knife and slice open my finger, squeezing several drops of blood, mixing it in. I don't know what I believe, but between my dreams and Fiona's faith, it's worth a try. I smear the concoction on the scars on my arms, then on my hip and thigh. I'm covered in the stuff and it's all on my pajamas. I laugh at myself, get a fresh pair of pajamas, and hop into the shower.

I take my time washing all the gunk off, and the room is steamy and pleasant when I'm done. I feel really tired all of a sudden, so I hurriedly dry off and wrap the towel around me, wiping the condensation from the mirror with my hand so I can brush my hair. My hand stops midway. I stare at myself in the mirror, at the flesh on the underside of my arm. I can't believe my eyes.

No marks, no scars.

I check my hip and my thigh. All of it is gone. The spiral, the Trinity knot. I feel sick now, and I vomit into the sink. I grab a pair of nail scissors out of the medicine cabinet and I stab my arm, retracing the pattern of the three-pronged

Trinity knot. It's crude, and I don't take my regular care, but when I'm finished I feel better. I collapse against the wall and slowly slide to the bathroom floor. The tile is cool on my bare legs.

There's no denying it now, as if I still could. It's real. The magic is real. And if I can heal myself, that means I can heal other people.

I can save my aunt.

33

pruдence

June 8, 1629
Eдinburgh

THEY TAKE HER away, like I knew they would.

We gather around the loch to witness her trial.

My father's eyes are glassy, his gaze blank. I told him what Primrose was. That she was wicked. That she needed seeing to. But he would hear none of it. He's gone soft in his old age. He did not even punish her when I told him about the boy. Well, I have made it right. The bishop has taken Primrose. I had no choice but to go to him, after Father would do nothing.

She will not drown; her magic is too strong. For a moment, I am doubtful, though. She goes under and does not resurface for a long moment. But then she bobs to the surface and is pulled from the water, alive and well. It is done.

She is a witch; there is no doubt now. My father collapses and I pull him to his feet, haul him home.

He and I are the same. We have both done such terrible things, and the doing has destroyed him. He is but a shadow of the imposing man he used to be, the one full of fire and brimstone and righteous fury. But still, he is my father.

Soon he will be the only family I have left.

34
heather

I WAIT UNTIL she's asleep. Along with all the other drugs she's taking, Aunt Abbie has a sedative that knocks her out.

I went to Robby's mom's shop and bought an incense burner and used my aunt's food dehydrator to dry the herbs. Now the bundle is ready. I light it and place it on her night table. I cut my hand and my blood sizzles as it drops onto the fire. I'm supposed to do this until the flame burns out, but after a few minutes my eyes get heavy. I can't keep them open.

I pass out.

For the next three days I can't move. I stay in bed and sleep. Robby visits and tries to get me to laugh, tells me jokes. But even his presence doesn't make me feel any better.

My aunt said she found me on the floor. She didn't mention the incense or the cut on my hand. She thinks I have the flu, but I know what it really is. I healed her and it took almost all I have.

When I finally get out of bed, I go into the kitchen and she's buzzing around, making lunch.

"Oh, Heather, I was just about to check on you. You look a lot better."

"So do you," I tell her.

"I feel fantastic. I have a date with the oncologist this afternoon, so we'll see what he says."

"I'm sure it will be good news." I sit at the table, still weak, and within moments Aunt Abbie has placed a cup of tea in front of me.

"Can you drop me off at Gram's?" I ask. I have an overwhelming urge to visit her.

"I dinnae know, love." She feels my head. "You seem better, but you were really down for the count."

"I miss her." I sip my tea. "And I am feeling much better."

"I know. And you didn't have a fever or anything. I guess as long as you don't hug or kiss her. I don't want her getting sick. She's not exactly a spring chicken."

"So I can go?"

"Aye. Get ready. We're leaving in ten."

I don't want my aunt to see how weak I actually am, so I

straighten up, sling my backpack, the grimoire safely inside, over my shoulder, and follow her down the stairs.

When Abbie drops me off, I head inside and rest on a chair for ten minutes before walking to Gram's room. She's mostly lucid, though she can't remember my name.

"Gram, I want to ask you about something. . . ." Where do I start? We've talked about witches before, but will she remember those conversations?

She looks me up and down, her eyes bright and aware. She seems to know what I need because she sighs and says, "You're having the dreams, aren't you?"

I nod. "Yes. At first it was just the one. . . ."

"The pyre. Watching a crowd as you"—she lowers her voice—"as you burn alive."

"So you have them too?"

"I used to. They nearly drove me mad. I thought I was done with that. For almost fifty years I've no' had a one. But now . . . Sometimes I think I'm young again, and I remember each and every agonizing moment of each and every dream."

"I'm sorry, Gram. That's horrible."

She sighs. "It cannae be helped. My mind is going, more each day. Have you heard the voices, too?"

I shake my head slowly. "I haven't, but sometimes . . . sometimes there are strange thoughts in my head. I don't know where they come from."

"It's them. The girls. They're trying to speak to you."

"But why?" I ask desperately.

"They've been at odds with each other for hundreds of years. Each feels wronged by the other. That kind of hatred doesn't just stop, not even if you die."

"But you got better. The dreams went away."

"Aye. Shortly after I turned seventeen. But before that, it was horrible. They were both in my head, telling me what to do. I couldnae think straight. And the nightmares—they just got worse and worse. Sometimes I couldnae tell what was real and what was just in my mind. It's like now, except no one expects a young girl to suffer from dementia. An old lady . . . well, they put me in here. Not that I blame them."

"Did you have the dreams about the cottage?" I ask.

She nods. "We'd go up there, on holiday."

"But you never removed the hearthstone? You never looked for proof you weren't crazy?"

"I was frightened. I'd go there sometimes and think about looking, but the dreams had ended. There was no point."

"Why do you think it all stopped?"

Gram shrugs. "I wish I knew for sure. Maybe because I reached the age that they died, so they didnae have the connection with me anymore."

"I thought Primrose was burned at the stake and Prudence lived on," I say.

Gram studies me. "Primrose . . . I havenae said that name in nearly fifty years. Yes, Primrose burned. That was the first dream, but it wasnae the nastiest. More will come, worse and worse. Prudence . . . well, her end is no' pleasant either. That's why there's so much hate between them. They each caused the other's death."

"So you believe it's all real?" I needed someone to say it aloud.

"I always have. There is magic in this world. Good and bad."

"I went up to the cottage last weekend," I tell her. "I had to look, had to know. I found the grimoire, exactly where it was in the dream."

Gram's face is pulled tight, a mixture of fear and hope. "May I see it? Did you bring it here?"

I open my backpack and hand her the cloth-wrapped book. She unwraps it, touching it reverently. "I think . . . I wasnae afraid to look because I was worried it wouldnae be there. I feared more that it would be. What would I do with this book? What would I be tempted to do?" She fingers the cover.

"Is this blood?"

"Yes. I'm sorry. I didn't mean to ruin it."

She grabs my arm. "Let me see the marks. Let me see what you have carved into your flesh."

"Gram, no." I pull away, nearly falling out of my chair.

"She got ahold of you right away. Didnae she? I always ignored the urge, the need. It feeds itself, you know. The more you do it, the more you want to."

"Did you ever try the healing magic?"

"Aye. I found a few others. They were my coven. Then more came, younger. That's how it is. The old give way to the young."

Gram is losing focus. "And who taught you?" I asked her.

"It was my father who was the MacNair. My mother had no idea about all this." She chortles. "You grandfather was a MacNair too, though very far removed. We used to joke before we were married how easy it would be for me . . . I didnae even have to change my last name."

"So it was your grandmother who practiced healing magic?" I prompt.

"Aye. She got funny when she was older too. She was sent away, to a place like this one." She sighs. "She was there until the day she died, though there wasnae much of *her* left. Not really. My grandmother, she wrestled with the same demons and chose the side of good, but I always wondered if I might go bad. I pretended I didnae have a talent for it, though I did. Couldnae fool the others, though; they saw right through me. I left the coven when I started to get fuzzy. Let the others get on without me. Their pasts were clear. They were no' haunted by their ancestors."

"Sheena Brodie's one, isn't she?" I ask. "She's a witch." She'd already told me as much.

She nods. "And there are a few others still around. When Abigail didnae have an ounce of magic in her, I was relieved. I thought it was all over."

"But you think I'm magical, that I have the ability to do what Sheena does? To make potions and salves and channel natural energy?" I hope it's true. I hope I saved my aunt.

"It's possible. You'd be smart no' to mess about with it, though, no' if you've already started to cut yourself. No good will come of it."

I reach for the book. "You should burn that," she tells me, handing it over.

"I can't."

"Then give it to someone with untainted blood." She studies me. "There may be a way to break free, but it's dangerous."

"What way?" I ask desperately.

"Fire." She closes her eyes. "The fire burned her beyond recognition. All she did, she did for love." When she opens her eyes, they're bright and fevered. "Dinnae let them talk you into doing it."

"Who, Gram? Doing what?"

"My coven. You could die and no' even break their spell. Those girls have their hooks in you and they're no' going to let go."

"Gram, please. I don't understand. Do you know what they want?"

"Aye." She looks at me, closes her eyes. "They want you. They're fighting over which one gets you."

35

primrose

THE WOODEN SLAB crushes the air from my chest. What breath I can recover comes in short, shallow gasps. If only all they wanted was for me to suffocate, it would already be over, this endless torture. No, what they want from me is far worse.

The panel of wood covers me from neck to knees. Most of its force bears down on my breast. Each breath is excruciating, and the coarse wood rubs my skin. I feel as if I am a piece of wet cloth being scrubbed on a washing board. No, not merely scoured, but squeezed until all that I am is wrung from my body.

"Confess!" the bishop screams as he places another stone on the panel. More weight to press my laboring lungs.

I fight as much as I can, but my arms and legs are held by metal shackles. The rest of me is pinned under the burden of the heavy wood and stones.

"Confess!" he yells again, inches from my face, his lips splattering spittle onto my cheek. A low moan escapes me. They have already found me guilty. What will a confession serve other than to validate their barbarity? I will not give them the pleasure.

He places another rock on the slab and now my breath comes in wheezing fits barely able to sustain me. This is the death I should have had in the loch, and it is a better death than the one that awaits me if I confess. I would rather suffocate than be put to the flames.

Lights flash in front of my eyes and I feel as if I am about to faint, but the bishop is a skilled torturer, and he removes one of the stones, relieves some of the pressure. Just enough air floods my lungs to keep me conscious.

"You know . . ." He no longer hovers over my face but whispers in my ear, soft and seductively, as if he has not spent the last few days tormenting me. "Witches are said to run in families. Perhaps I should call on yours. I wonder if your sister has the same marks as you. . . ."

Even with my limbs numb, I can feel his caress on my arm. I close my eyes and try to shake the memory of his cruel hands on me when he checked me for signs of witchcraft. His glee as he recorded every mole. His delight to find I was no virgin. I vomited after he violated me, too broken even to cry.

I cannae let that happen to her. I use what little breath

I have left in my body to whisper through my cracked and bleeding lips.

"I confess."

Once again the bishop is in my face. "You confess to practicing witchcraft?"

"Yes."

"And to communing with Satan?"

I can barely exhale, so I nod my answer.

"And to fornicating with Satan's minions?"

I nod again.

"And you will sign your name to a full confession?" he asks, almost gleefully.

"Yes!" I rasp. "Yes to it all." I want it done.

The bishop looks over his shoulder. "Take her back to her cell. See that she gets water and food. I do not want to see her perish before we can arrange her punishment."

The weight is slowly lifted from my chest, offering blissful relief. Hands eventually grab me and drag me to my prison, where I collapse into a heap, resting my head against the hard stone ground. It smells of piss and death.

It will be the pyre for me. What have I done?

My fate was already determined. At least this way, I save her. That is all that matters now.

36

heather

MY AUNT IS still sick. I feel the crushing weight of dread, as bad as my dream of Primrose's torture. Why are my scars gone, but my aunt's cancer remains?

I look at the grimoire on my nightstand. Its ancient pages mock me. I had such hope.

"So Felipe thinks I should come visit him over Christmas break, but I'm not sure I want to make that kind of commitment . . . ," Fiona is saying. "Hello, Heather?"

"Hmmm?"

"You weren't even listening," she accuses me.

"Sure I was. Spanish boy with the dreamy eyes is madly in love with you now, and you just want to use him. . . ."

She laughs. "Come on, what's up?"

I sigh. "Do you think the love potion worked?"

"Absolutely."

"So if I were to tell you that the magic worked for me too, you'd believe me?"

"What, you gave Robby a love potion?" She throws back her head, her curls shaking. "I hate to tell you, he'd already fallen for you."

"No, not a love potion." I debate how much to tell her. "I had this scar on my arm and I made a healing salve that I read about in the book and now the scar is gone. Not faded. It's like it never existed."

Fiona stares at me. "That's amazing. Why didn't you tell me?"

"I tried the same thing on my aunt to cure her cancer and she said she felt better, but she's still sick."

Fiona thinks about it. "Well, cancer's not some small scar. Cancer is huge."

"Yeah, and it took a lot out of me. After I did it, I was completely drained. I know my aunt said I had the flu, but really, I think it's what happens when you try to cure something like that. It steals all your energy. And it didn't even work."

"Maybe you don't have enough healing power. What if two people did it? I could be with you next time."

"You think that would work?"

"My blood worked in the love potion. Why do you think your blood is so bloody special? I bet my blood is just as powerful. I can help save Abbie's life."

I sit up. "You'd do that for me?"

"For you and your aunt? Don't be stupid. Of course I would."

"But what if we both just pass out and it still doesn't work?" I ask.

"Fair point." Her eyes brighten. "Let's get Asha to come and monitor us."

"Asha will think we are absolutely bonkers."

"I dinnae know. You heard her and all that stuff about her grandparents. And even if she doesnae believe us, she will after your aunt gets cured."

"Okay, but I still need to recover a bit. What about this weekend?"

"Works for me."

Robby comes over the next night to keep me company. We sit on the couch and watch TV while my aunt putters around the flat, keeping an eye on us. I didn't tell her that Robby and I were dating, but she seems to sense the change in us. The electricity between us. Eventually her meds kick in and she gives up on chaperoning us and goes to bed.

Robby leans in; his breath tickles my skin. He kisses my ear, my cheek, my lips. I'm no longer weak or drained from my "illness." Instead, I feel powerful. My nerves are on fire. Before I know it, I've pulled off his shirt. My aunt is just in the other room; she could wake up and walk in at any time, but I don't care.

Robby hesitates, then lifts my shirt over my head. My

necklace falls back down and rests on my chest. I'm acutely aware that I'm sitting here in my bra, suddenly chilled. His hand rubs my arm, and too late, I try to pull away.

"Heather, what's that?" he asks, his head jerking up. His fingers caress my fresh carving, the Trinity knot.

"Oh, this," I try to sound casual. "It's just a tat I want. My mom wouldn't let me, so I did it myself."

He lifts my arm to examine the wound. "It looks fresh. . . . Did you cut this into your skin?"

He's got a solid grip on my arm, but I twist it out of his grasp. "What's the big deal?" I ask, my voice filled with irritation that I hope covers my fear.

"Heather, if you want a tattoo, get henna, or use a Sharpie, but why would you cut yourself?"

I glare at him. "It's my body. I can do whatever I want with it."

"I'm not saying you can't, it's just . . ."

And there it is, what I've dreaded. That look. He thinks I'm a total freak.

"This was a bad idea," I say.

"A bad idea for me to come over, or a bad idea that we're . . ." He stops, looks at me.

I can't meet his eyes. "Both."

"Heather . . . I . . ." He reaches for me, but I scoot away, off the couch, grabbing my shirt. I pull it over my head.

"You can leave now. We'll pretend this never happened."

He stands. "You're being . . ." He looks confused and more than a little angry.

"What? What am I being?" I shout, no longer caring if my aunt hears. "Crazy? Unreasonable? A freak?"

"You're being a bloody bitch," he snaps, then closes his mouth fast. Anger floods my body. I could slap him.

"Nice. And you're a complete twat." What right does he have to call me a bitch? A sudden urge comes over me to claw out his eyes. *He deserves it, the brute. You dinnae need him.* I bite back the feelings.

"Just go."

He puts on his shirt and leaves without another word. I go to my room and cry into the pillow. Why did I think I had a chance at being normal?

37

prudence

June 10, 1629
Edinburgh

I HEAR HER screams, but I do naught.

I sit outside the church basement in the dark alley, alone in the shadows. The moon is only a sliver tonight, barely enough light by which to see the cobblestones. A shady-looking figure hurries past me. I do not fear him. I am one with the darkness, and tonight there is no creature that lurks there who is more fearsome than I.

Another scream. I revel in them, and they repulse me.

It is my fault.

It is my triumph.

38

heather

"Wow, THAT SOUNDS like it escalated quickly," Asha says.

"Yeah, no kidding," Fiona adds. We're all sitting on my bed, waiting for my aunt to go to sleep.

"I just was so angry with him," I say. I told them Robby and I had a fight, what we said, but not what it was about. "And then he called me a bitch . . ."

"Yeah, that's not cool," Fiona tells me. "Even though it sounds like you were acting like one." I give her a look. "But I'm still absolutely on your side."

"Thanks," I tell her.

"So that's it? You and Robby were together for a week and now you're not even going to be friends?" Asha asks.

I shrug.

Fiona's phone buzzes and she glances at it. "Felipe," she tells us.

Asha sighs. "Right, the boy who loves you because you gave him a magic sex potion. That's logical."

"Yes, when I think love, I also think logic," Fiona says.

I glance at the clock. It's almost ten. My aunt has been out for an hour. She should be dead to the world, especially since I convinced her to take an extra sedative to help her sleep.

"Are you guys ready?" I ask. Earlier I gathered the herbs and dried and bundled them, readying them to be burned.

My friends nod. "Let's go, then," I say. "And, Fiona, remember that a large part of this is intent. You have to will Aunt Abbie to be healed."

"And my job is just to make sure neither of you bleeds to death? I really don't like this," Asha says.

"If it was someone you loved who was sick, we'd do the same for you," Fiona tells her.

"No, I would bring them to a doctor or the hospital."

"Abbie's been to see doctors, and she practically lives in the hospital lately. They haven't helped her."

"But this will?" Asha asks, motioning to the herbs. I know it looks crazy.

"Well, it cannae hurt," Fiona says.

"Fine." Asha relents. "But I have the paramedics on speed dial."

We sneak into my aunt's room, but there's really no need. She's completely out. I light the herbs and place the bowl near her head. Fiona and I stand shoulder to shoulder.

"Ready?" I ask. She nods, her red curls bouncing.

I take the knife and slice her hand. She hisses and tries to pull away, but I firmly place her hand over the bowl. "That bloody hurt."

"Think healing thoughts," I whisper.

"Right." She takes a deep breath and closes her eyes. "Healing thoughts."

I cut my own hand and hold it over the bowl. *Please get better. Please get better. Please get better.*

I begin to get tired, and Fiona sways next to me.

"Enough," Asha says.

"No, not yet." I feel it more this time. My aunt's body is repairing itself, but just the damage from the chemo, not the cancer itself. It's like our health is going from me and Fiona into her. We're connected by blood. "Are you okay, Fiona?" I ask.

"Just a wee bit dizzy. Do you think it's working?"

"Yes. Can't you feel it?" I ask. She's really pale.

"No, I just feel . . . like rubbish."

"That's your energy going into her," I tell her. If Fiona can't feel it, I need to stay awake and in charge, to make sure Aunt Abbie is completely healed. That means I need to give less of myself, which will only work if Fiona gives more.

"Can you . . . Are you up for a little more?"

She closes her eyes and bites her lip. "Aye, what's another pint?"

I take the knife and in one smooth motion slash her wrist. She gasps, but doesn't move to leave. I didn't mean to cut so deeply, but I can feel it working. Still, it isn't enough. Light-headed, I slice my own wrist. I can feel the blackness beckoning, but I fight it. My aunt is not healed yet.

Asha is screaming now, but it sounds far away. I ignore her. Fiona and I are locked in the spell. I'm determined to heal my aunt, no matter the price.

The last thing I remember is my aunt's face before me, her look of pure horror as I stand over her with a knife, bleeding.

She is frightened. Not *for* me.

Of me.

39

prudence

June 13, 1629
Edinburgh

I WALK ALONG the cobbled street, pushing my way through the crowd. Ducking into an alley, I hurry around the back of a building and emerge again, past the bulk of the onlookers. I know this city better than I know myself; it sings to me. I love every nook and cranny, the good with the bad. Even the smell of the city is alive. Already, smoke hangs heavily in the air, as does a scent less recognizable: rage. They are angry at the witch and have come to see her burn.

I reach the inner crowd and make my way through, closer to the blaze. A new smell envelops me, one of searing flesh. A man next to me turns to the side and retches. Some do not have the constitution for justice. I step past him and push my way to the front.

There she is, bound to the stake, her legs already ablaze. Her screams could wake the dead, and the bishop is spouting some nonsense that she is trying to communicate with the devil himself. As if only a witch would scream whilst on fire. I am jostled, and the look I shoot the noblewoman who's pushed me makes her wilt. I turn my attention back to the pyre. I will not be distracted.

I watch every moment of her suffering. Drink it in. I cannot look away. So many emotions bubble under my skin: anger, vindication, jealousy, even a hint of regret.

I stare at her and wonder if she will see me, but she looks to the sky, as if for comfort. Many of the crowd back away, their resolve weakening with the hard truth of a witch's pyre. But I move forward. I need her to see me. I need her to know.

Finally, her eyes find mine, and I hold my head high as our gazes lock.

The pain on her face is momentarily erased by a look of stunned betrayal. Then the light goes out of her eyes altogether as the flames consume her soul.

Once she is dead, the crowd completely loses interest. Justice has been served: Satan's handmaiden has been slain.

The bishop and I are the only ones who stay until the bitter end. Until the flames die and all that is left are the charred remains of a witch.

40

primrose

June 13, 1629
Edinburgh

BLACK SMOKE SCALDS my lungs.

A crowd is gathered, their faces lit by the flames, but also ablaze with the joyous anticipation of my punishment. A few are pious men and women who have come to see God's justice done. Most have come to witness the spectacle.

They have come to see me burn.

One girl pushes her way to the front of the crowd. The sight of her makes my heart soar. She will save me. I know she will. Hope floods my body, and I trick myself into believing that the flames have been extinguished. A new bout of pain pushes that thought from my head.

When I focus once again on the girl, my faith is dashed; my heart plummets back to the earth, shattering against the cold, unloving stone. I realize that she isnae here to save me.

The last thing I see is her look of pure, triumphant joy.

Hate fills my body as I, at last, pass into darkness.

There is no more pain, and with the lack of physical feeling, emotion rushes in to fill the void. My whole being abhors her. I am hatred.

I shall get my revenge.

41

heather

I DREAM OF fire.

I wake in an unfamiliar bed in an empty hospital room. Bandages are wrapped tightly around one wrist, an IV in the other. I clumsily pull out the needle, ignoring the small trail of blood that flows down my arm. My stuff is in a bag on a chair, and I stand to reach it. Woozy, I lean against the bed. Each movement takes a lot out of me. I slowly slip out of my hospital gown and into clothes.

I step out into the hall and find Asha sitting in a chair, her head in her hands.

"Asha?"

Her head snaps up. "Heather! You shouldn't be up!"

"Where's Fiona?"

Her eyes drift to another room and I see her lying in bed, her mother and sister standing over her.

"She was worse off than you," Asha says. "She needed a blood transfusion and . . ." Her face collapses into tears. "She's in a coma. What the hell were you thinking?" she asks. "I should never have let you two go through with it."

"It's not your fault," I tell her.

"No, Heather, it's yours." She stands. "I didn't know what to tell them, so I said I was in the other room and I came in and saw what was going on and I called an ambulance." She looks at her feet, ashamed.

"I'll—I'll think of something to say to them."

"You'd better think fast," she tells me frostily. "Your aunt is downstairs getting coffee. She called your parents. They're coming."

My parents are going to have me committed. And poor Fiona. I look in the window. Mary is crying softly, while her mother looks like she's aged a decade overnight. It's all my fault.

"I am in so much trouble."

"So am I!" Asha yells. "My parents are really angry. They only let me stay because I thought you both were going to die. . . ." She closes her eyes, squeezing out tears that drop down her cheek.

"Asha, I'm so sorry."

She sniffles and wipes her face. "I'm not the one you should apologize to." She grabs her bag and heads down the hall to the elevator bank.

I eye Fiona's room, taking a moment before gathering the strength to open the door and step in. I don't think I'm supposed to be here, but I have to explain. Mary, Fiona's stepsister, spots me first, her eyes wide. She's scared of me.

"Mrs. Darrow," I whisper. Her eyes focus on me, and the look on her face turns to one of pure anger. In three strides she stands in front of me, lifts her hand, and slaps me hard across the face.

My eyes water and my cheek burns. "I'm so sorry," I whimper.

"You are playing with powers you do not understand," she tells me. "You had no right to drag Fiona into this."

My mouth hangs open, and I don't know what to say, when strong hands grab my shoulders and pull me back into my room. It's Robby's mom, Sheena Brodie.

"It's all right, love," Sheena tells me. "We'll figure this all out."

Sheena lets me cry softly on her shoulder. When I'm done, she wipes my face. "That's enough of that, now," she says.

My hand goes to my neck. "I lost the necklace you gave me," I tell her. "I'm sorry." It's such a small thing, something stupid for me to focus on instead of everything else.

"Oh, love, that's all right. The necklace was just a prop. The Trinity knot is supposed to help you focus your energies, you know. Not that you need any help with that, do you?" She sighs. "I was going to watch you, see if you showed any talent. I had no idea how powerful you already are."

I sniffle and look at the floor, but she holds my chin and makes me look into her eyes.

"I need you to tell me everything."

And I do. I tell her about the dreams, about the visions,

about the cutting, about my grandma, about the book. I tell her everything, and it feels so good to get it all off my chest.

"Don't you think if I could have cured Abbie, I would have?" she asks. "She is beyond our help. The only thing that would have worked is a life for a life. That's why you were so knackered after your first attempt."

"But this time . . . I'm tired, but not nearly as bad as before," I tell her.

She nods. "And Fiona's in that hospital bed, unconscious."

I tell her how I felt during, how I could feel the health draining from me and Fiona, how I could focus it. I took more from Fiona than I did from myself.

"To save my aunt would have killed Fiona," I say horrified at the revelation.

"Aye."

I shake my head. "I didn't know. I didn't understand."

"And that's why playing with Blood Magic is dangerous. Now tell me more about these sisters, the ones who haunt you."

I tell her everything I know. About the thoughts that are not my own. "I want to be free of them," I say.

"Go back to your aunt and have her take you home. Burn that book."

"That's what Gram said to do. Will that work?"

"I dinnae know for sure, but a grimoire is a very powerful object. Destroying it might stop them."

"Gram said there was another way. That her old coven could help me."

"Did she tell you how?" she asks quietly.

"No, she just said it was dangerous. That I could die."

Sheena nods. "Burn the grimoire. Perhaps that will be enough."

"Will burning the book help Fiona?"

Sheena shakes her head. "It is not that easy to undo Blood Magic gone wrong. She's beyond your help now. There's nothing you can do for her. She needs to rest, and hopefully she will recover."

"Tell her family . . ." I don't know what to say. "I'm just so sorry."

"They know," she says before slipping out. "But perhaps you should let them be for now. Go home. Burn the book. Try to rest."

When my aunt walks in with coffee, she hugs me. Her eyes are red and puffy. "Why would you want to kill yourself?" she asks.

"I wasn't trying to kill myself," I tell her. I don't know how to explain in a way that will make sense to her. "It was an accident."

"The cuts were self-inflicted. The doctors said—"

I look at my aunt. I want to tell her the truth. I told Sheena Brodie everything, but my aunt has no idea about Blood Magic. If I try to explain now, I'll sound absolutely insane.

"We were playing around, trying to make a movie, a horror film," I interrupt. "It got out of hand. It was stupid."

She looks me up and down. "You werenae trying to kill yourself?"

"No! Please, let's go home."

"I'll go get a nurse and see if we can get out of here."

"And my parents?" I ask.

"You scared them half to death. They'll be here tomorrow."

After an hour I'm released from the hospital. I have to talk to a psychiatrist and convince him I'm not insane or suicidal. He ends up believing that Fiona and I were attempting to make a film. I told them we'd watched a movie about witches and it inspired me. I wanted a scene in which we would hold a ritual. I wanted it to be realistic, so I suggested we cut ourselves for real, just a little, not understanding the risk. I lied that I hadn't known how sharp the knives were, how dangerous. When he asks to see the video, I say we never even got to that part, it went so wrong so fast. Better that he thinks I'm stupid than insane.

They agree to release me into my aunt's care. At the flat she refuses to let me out of her sight. I don't blame her. I show her the book and tell her it's partially what gave Fiona and me the idea to cut ourselves.

"We thought it looked like something a witch would use, and after we saw that movie, I thought we could use it to make an awesome prop in our scene." I tell her I want to burn it as a therapeutic release. I feel bad about lying, but I'm in so deep, what's a few more lies?

Aunt Abbie grabs the book out of my hands and throws it in the sink. She rummages through some drawers, finds a bottle of lighter fluid and pours the liquid on the ancient grimoire. She hands me the matches.

"Go ahead, if this will make you feel better. Get rid of

the bloody thing, if it's why you thought you should cut yourself and nearly kill your friend." Her voice is hard, but her face is soft—defeated, almost.

My hands tremble as I light a match, letting it burn nearly down to my fingers before it goes out. Aunt Abbie just watches me. I shakily light another, and I only let it burn for a moment before I throw it onto the book. The grimoire lights up in a spectacular pyre.

My family history, my magical inheritance, all gone in a puff of smoke. Generations of women have recorded their knowledge, and in an instant, I've destroyed their legacy. I let out a sob and my aunt hugs me.

"Do you feel any better, love?"

I shake my head. If anything, I feel worse. I reach in to pick up the blackened tatters.

"Heather, careful, that's still hot," my aunt tells me.

I remove my hand, but I'm not burned. "I didn't actually touch the fire," I tell her, though I did. I look at my hand. No burns. The skin isn't even red from the heat.

We watch the blaze die down. And then, just before we go to bed, my aunt turns on the tap and drowns the last licks of flame.

42

prudence

September 9, 1629
Edinburgh

I AM AT the top of Arthur's Seat. The cloudy sky is starless, and all I have is the moon's reflection to show me how high I am, how far I have to fall.

I have no recollection of how I got here. The wind and rain have plastered my nightdress to my belly, the bulge clear for all to see. It was she who brought me here. I thought I'd be rid of her, but she haunts me even now.

As if in answer to my suspicions, a voice inside my head tells me:

Jump.

Four little letters, but so powerful. I listen.

I cry out against it. It would be so easy to end my life, to be reunited with Primrose, but I cannae. Even with all the wickedness that I have done, I dinnae want to leave this world. I want to live.

My hand goes to my belly. What chance does this child have, begot of hate and jealousy? What chance do I have when I am discovered?

The wind whispers again.

Jump.

It takes everything I have to back away from the ledge, to make my way home, one heavy footstep at a time. She will not have me, or my child. Primrose willnae win.

I have taken her life, and I shall live it as best I can.

43

heather

WHEN I WAKE, I'm on top of Arthur's Seat, in my pajamas.
The cold air flows around me, and I can barely feel my feet.
I look down at the drop.

Jump. And then an echo: *Jump.*

I lean forward on my numb toes. What is there to live
for? My family thinks I'm insane. My aunt is dying. My
gram is no longer herself. And Asha hates me for what happened with Fiona. What if Fiona doesn't wake up? And if
she does, how will she ever forgive me?

Tears fall down my face. *I no longer even have my sister.*

The thought breaks me out of my trance. I never had a
sister.

I scuttle back from the edge, scraping my heels and

leaving a streak of blood on the craggy rocks. I crouch and hug my knees. Burning the book did nothing. These thoughts are still here, whispering, haunting me.

They are not my own.

When I can't take the cold any longer, I make my way down the hill, slowly and carefully. My feet are a wreck, the skin scraped and raw, but they're so numb, I can barely feel the pain.

I limp down the final steps and out through the park, hugging my arms to my sides. A cab pulls up beside me.

"All right, love?" the cabbie calls. "Had a rough night?"

"You have no idea."

"Need the coppers?" he asks, glancing down at my bare feet.

"No . . . I just need to get home."

"Hop in, I'll take you."

Relief floods through me, a chance to sit in a warm car. But then I frown. "I don't have any money," I say.

"It's slow anyway. . . . I'll get you where you need to go."

"Thank you," I breathe, getting into the cab. I hope karma is real, because this man should get a buttload of good karma.

"Where to?" he asks.

I glance at the clock. Four in the morning. My aunt may still be sleeping. I could sneak in; she'd never know I was gone. But what would that solve? I'd be with my parents on the next flight home, stuck in an institution with two ghosts fighting in my head.

"New Town," I tell him. I give him the address. A short ride later, I'm standing on the doorstep of Sheena Brodie's house. I need her help. I need answers.

I ring the doorbell, then knock loudly on the door, then ring the doorbell again.

"All right, all right," a familiar voice calls. The door opens, and Robby looks me up and down. "Heather, what the bloody hell . . ." He eyes my dirt-stained pajamas and ruined feet. "Heather, what happened?"

"I need to see your mother, now," I tell him. He reaches out to me and I collapse into his arms with a sob.

"It didn't work," I tell Sheena desperately as she cleans my feet. "I burned the book, but they're still here. They won't be happy until I'm dead or insane."

"What is she on about?" Robby asks, but Sheena just shushes him.

"Robby, I need you to go to the hospital and fetch Janet Darrow. Send her here and tell her you'll stay with Fiona. Make sure she knows I said it's important."

"She's not going to leave Fiona's side . . . ," Robby tells her.

"She'll come if I ask her to," Sheena tells him. Robby doesn't move.

"I'm not leaving Heather." He puts his arm around me. "I'm sorry for what I said. . . ."

"Me too," I whisper.

Sheena puts her hands on her hips. "Robby, if you want to help Heather, go. Now."

Robby kisses my forehead and leaves.

"What now?" I ask.

"Rest," Sheena tells me, offering me a hot drink that knocks me right out.

44

pruдence

March 1, 1630
Edinburgh

THIS TIME, WHEN I visit him, I bring no potions. Only myself.

He has been drinking heavily; I can smell the whisky on his breath as he answers the door. The look he gives me is full of hatred, but he allows me in. That is all I want, to speak with him.

He sits heavily on a chair and pours himself another drink, swallowing it in one gulp. He rests his bleary eyes on me. "What do you want?"

"I have come to make an offer."

"I do not deal with the devil," he tells me. "And if the devil is real, you are he."

"I . . ." I pause, unsure of how to convince him. "I had your child," I blurt out. "From that night we lay together . . ."

His hand stops halfway to the bottle. "You are a liar."

"I am no' lying. I had a child . . . a girl. My father has taken her, has disowned me. But if I were to return with a husband, he would accept me again. We need not tell him . . . what you are."

Jonas laughs hollowly. "Primrose cared not that I was born a Jew. My parents fled Spain and thought to have a life here, only to find more harassment and persecution. She would have been my wife, to hell with religion."

"And now I can be your wife." I reach for his hand and it trembles in my grasp. "I look like her. You can pretend I am her. I wouldnae mind."

He whips his hand away from me. "You come to me in her guise and whisper temptations. But who would marry the devil's whore?"

"You. We have a child together. Primrose would want—"

"Dinnae say her name!" he yells, standing. He throws the near-empty bottle at me. I duck and it smashes against the wall. "You are not her. You are nothing like her."

He rushes me and I am not quick enough to run from him, nor am I strong enough to break his grasp. His fingers clutch my arms. His hands are so strong, they could crush my bones.

It was very stupid to come here.

"I will leave at once," I tell him, my voice squeaking.

"You will, will you?" he asks, and I can see the malice in his eyes. "You'll come here, ruin my life, and leave? Just like that?"

His hands crawl up my arms to my shoulders, and his long fingers encircle my neck.

"Please," I beg.

"I know it was you," he tells me, his face dark, spittle flying from his lips. "You named her a witch."

He squeezes, and I gasp for breath. I claw at his hands, at his face, but he doesnae let go. Lights flash before my eyes; his face, red and angry, takes up my entire range of vision. Before I pass out I hear a crunch, and still he doesnae loosen his hold. He doesnae release his grasp until the landlord finds us days later and pries my cold, dead body from him.

45

heather

WHEN I WAKE, I have no idea where I am. I sit up and spot Sheena speaking with an older woman with long, frizzy gray hair. It all comes back to me: Fiona. Primrose and Prudence.

Sheena brings the older woman over and introduces her. "This is Ruth." Ruth's pale blue eyes study me.

Fiona's mother is there too. I try to avoid her gaze.

"What's going on?" I ask Sheena.

"This is my coven," she explains.

"You're all witches?"

"Wiccan, healers, witches . . . names are irrelevant," Ruth says.

"Do you know how to help me?"

"We havenae seen this before, a person haunted by two spirits who wish to do her harm," Sheena tells me.

"I don't think it's that exactly. . . . They don't want to harm me," I say, feeling foolish. I'm battered but not broken. I try to explain. "They hate each other. So much. I'm just in the cross fire. I can hear them both . . . feel them both. They've been fighting for so long, and they each want to win."

Ruth is watching me. "Win what?"

"They see me—all the MacNair girls, really—as a prize to be won."

Sheena nods. "I'm glad Abbie avoided all this. It's not often a MacNair is born with no talent for magic."

"We should have told her anyway," Ruth cuts in. "We shouldnae have left her ignorant. Now Anne MacNair is too far gone and it's just been us for years." Again she looks at me, assessing me. "We need new blood."

"Anne wanted it that way," Sheena snaps. "We arenae here to strengthen our coven, we're here to help Heather."

Before Ruth can respond, a phone rings, and Fiona's mom pulls out her cell while Ruth shoots her a dirty look.

"I am not going to ignore a call that might have something to do with my daughter," she says, answering the phone while Ruth looks incredibly annoyed and Sheena looks slightly embarrassed.

"Oh, thank you," Mrs. Darrow breathes into her phone. "Fiona, I'm so sorry I'm not there. Robby came and got me . . ." She pauses. "He said what?" She listens for a bit, then walks over and hands me the phone. "My daughter insists on speaking with you."

I shakily take the phone from her hands. "Fiona?" I say her name hesitantly, almost afraid it's not really her. But the voice that comes through is most definitely Fiona's.

"Oh, bloody hell, Heather. What am I doing in hospital?"

I let out a sob, full of relief and guilt. "I am so sorry. I didn't mean for this to happen."

"Oh, dinnae be so dramatic. You didnae exactly twist my arm. I volunteered."

"But I didn't stop it when I felt you were getting hurt. . . ."

"Look, I know my mum is on the warpath right now, and Robby told me that you're a total mess about this, but I dinnae blame you."

"Thank you," I say, though I don't feel any better.

"I'm not dead, and that's the main thing. And I basically have a sympathy card to play for the rest of the summer. Plus I get a hot boy spending the night with me." I hear Robby laugh in the background. "And I'm going to call Felipe, so I'll have two hot boys. . . . Hmmm, whatever will we do?" Her voice is weak, but her tone is as cheeky as ever.

"You don't hate me?" I ask.

"Dinnae be stupid," she says. "Let me talk to my mum." Her voice is small, and I can hear how tired she really is.

I hand the phone back over, a weight lifted from my chest. If only Primrose and Prudence could forgive each other.

"I need to speak with them," I say.

"The ghosts?" Ruth asks. She glances around the group, nodding as if to say *I told you so.*

"Yes. Can't we do a séance or something?"

"This isnae a movie, Heather," Sheena says. "Those girls had great power in life, and they have great power in death. They reach you through that power, but for you to contact them . . ." She stops.

"I've communed with the spirit world," Ruth says quietly, her voice traveling through the room like a current of air through a graveyard.

"How?" I ask.

Janet places her hand on my shoulder. I know she hasn't forgiven me, but with Fiona on the mend, she's at least stifled her hostilities. "This is what your gram warned you about. The danger. Because the only way for you to talk to the dead is to *be* dead."

"If that's true, how did *you* do it?" I ask Ruth.

"My coven killed me," she tells me, staring at me with those cold, icy blue eyes. "They kept my body on the edge of life. Then they brought me back."

"We almost lost you," Sheena says. "We also had Anne then. She was the most powerful of us all."

"I don't care about the risks. I want to do it," I tell them. "I need to do it."

"Love, you told me your grandmother had these visions . . . these dreams, but they stopped when she was seventeen. That's not too far off. Why not just wait?" Sheena asks.

"They're driving me to the edge," I tell them. "I'll either end up dead or in an institution. And even if I get past this, like Gram did, what do I have to look forward to?"

Sheena looks unconvinced. "You're a mother," I tell her.

"How can I let my children inherit this curse? How could I ever be happy knowing that one day my daughter or my granddaughter will be tortured by this?"

"And if you die for good?" Sheena asks. "How am I to explain that to your aunt, to your family? How am I to live with that on my conscience?"

"Then don't let me die," I say. Surprisingly, my voice doesn't shake. I don't want to die, even temporarily, and this whole plan sounds insane, but no less so than living like I have been.

"It willnae be pleasant, Heather," Mrs. Darrow says. "You're a Blood Witch now, so it's the water for you. You have to drown. We'll pump your chest and try to breathe life back into your body, but there's no guarantee."

"Why did you do it?" I ask Ruth.

"My daughter died in a car accident when she was five." Ruth's hard exterior cracks and I see the pain in her watery eyes. "Her father died too. I had to put her soul to rest."

"Then you understand," I whisper.

"Aye. But when I saw her, she was mangled. Alone and terrified. I was drawn to that place, wanted to stay there with her. I almost didnae make it back. Death is not an easy thing to overcome."

"You're not going to scare me out of this," I tell her, swallowing my concerns past the lump in my throat.

Ruth stares at me a while longer. "We have to let the girl decide," she declares. "It's her life. It's her choice. And she'll need us all to bring her back."

Janet looks me over. "Fiona will kill you if you die."

"I know," I say, letting out a small, scared laugh. She

leans in and hugs me. "I am sorry for what I dragged her into."

She wipes the tears from my eyes. "I wanted her to be free of all of this and was relieved when she didnae show a talent for healing. I never thought she'd find out about Blood Magic."

She holds my shoulders, and we all look to Sheena. Her eyes are closed, and for a moment I think she will object, but when she opens them there's purpose in her gaze.

"Okay, then. Let's prepare."

46

heather

I SIT NAKED in a bathtub filled with lukewarm water. Herbs float on the surface—cinnamon sticks and basil, turmeric and arrowroot and garlic—as if I'm part of a stew. The coven surround me, Janet and Ruth on either side and Sheena at my head.

This should be beyond awkward, but I'm too scared to feel anything else.

"Are you ready?" Sheena asks.

I try to sound confident. "Yes."

"Truly?" Sheena wants me to be sure.

"It's the girl's choice," Ruth says once again.

"I'm ready," I tell them.

I lean back. Three pairs of strong hands gently push me

down and hold me there. Ruth and Janet pin my arms, and Sheena holds down my forehead. At first I am unafraid; the water feels warm and comforting, like a liquid reprieve from reality. But it doesn't take long for me to feel uncomfortable. My lungs burn, eager for air. Still I hold my breath.

Then the panic sets in.

I've died twice already, by burning and by strangulation. But those were dream deaths. Secondhand experiences.

This death is real. This death is mine.

I try to flail my arms, try to break free, but the women have me held secure. There are three of them and one of me, and I feel weak and alone. Even kicking does nothing. I know I must die, but I fight for life.

What have I done? What if this doesn't work? I've placed my life in the hands of these women, one of whom I just met and two of whom have lied to me my whole life. I want to signal that I've changed my mind, but there is no way to let them know. I let out the last of the air in my lungs, the bubbles releasing in a silent, watery scream.

Finally, I can no longer control my lungs and I involuntarily take a breath of liquid.

It feels like I have inhaled molten lava, and my whole body fights against the wrongness of it. The water is forced out, but with the next intake it seems less hurtful, more . . . almost normal. That water I leave in my lungs. There is no point in expelling it. It is now a part of me. I no longer need air.

I am dead.

47

heather

EVERYWHERE THERE IS haze, but I am walking, so there must be ground beneath my feet. Yes, I can smell it: the earthy peat and the crisp air, the soft scents of the Highlands.

The mist begins to clear and I see the landscape now, rolling hills covered in beautiful purple heather. The sky is so blue.

"I was happiest here," someone says over my shoulder. I spin and find Primrose watching me. Her skin is burned black, charred and cracking. There is no hair on her head, there are no eyes in her sockets. She is a husk.

I take a step back. Ruth warned me, but I didn't understand. I make myself look at the scorched figure. "I saw. You and Prudence . . ."

"Do not say her name," she warns. Her mouth forms the words through blistered lips. Her voice is surprisingly strong. "She betrayed me."

"She did. But . . ." The landscape stays the same as laughter breaks through the silence. Two identical girls chase each other, squealing gleefully at their game.

"She took my life," Primrose says darkly. The girls disappear. We are no longer in the Highlands, but in a narrow alley in Edinburgh. "She took away the earth and the sky and instead gave me a stone cage."

"It was Father who moved us to the city." Prudence appears next to Primrose. She speaks to me, not to her sister. Her neck is bent at a strange angle; angry red handprints encircle her throat. Her eyes are bloodshot and bulge from her skull. "I told him what our mother was doing. It was a mistake, a child's folly. I didnae know he would take her life."

"Did she no' ken the bishop would take mine?" Though they stand side by side, they address only me. "Was that no' the plan? To steal my life and my happiness?"

Even through their injuries, I can see that they have identical looks of anger on their faces, identical looks of hatred. "Was I no' allowed happiness as well?" Prudence shouts. "She would have eloped, left me alone with our beast of a father, left me . . ." Her voice quiets. ". . . left me."

"My life was moving onward, and Prudence wished for it to stay still."

Prudence wheels on her, looks at her for the first time. "Did you ask me? Did you consult with me? No, you had no' a care for me, so why should I have a care for you? You deserved what fate you received."

"As did you," Primrose shouts back. "You thought to steal my man, to have the life that I wanted. Well, I whispered in Jonas's ear, and he was only too happy to take your life in return."

"There was a baby," I cut in, and the girls' attention snaps back to me, each looking surprised that I am here. I try to channel Dr. Casella, use all the therapy sessions I've attended. "Prudence had a baby with the man you loved," I tell Primrose. "And that child eventually had a child, and on and on, until there was me. Do you want to torture us all?"

"I care not for the well-being of her progeny," Primrose spits.

"But what about Jonas? What about the love you shared?" I ask. She glowers. "You were willing to care for Prudence's child as your own because it had a part of Jonas as well."

"She would have taken my child," Prudence says as she rubs the welts on her neck. "She would have stolen my babe from me and left me with nothing."

"And that's why you fight over us?" I ask them. "You fight for control over the lives of any MacNair girl left. Why only the girls?"

"Not all can see us," Primrose says. "Only women have the talent, and only those with magic in their blood. I wanted Jonas's child. We were meant to have a family together." She no longer sounds so angry, and I notice she looks at me through fully formed eyes, not just dark sockets. She now has random patches of light blond hair on her head. Am I winning her over?

"And you," I tell Prudence. "Didn't you feel any love toward your child?"

"Of course, but Father took her from my breast. He called me unfit, and worse besides. He left me and took away the babe." Her anger is deflated now. "I thought if I was married and respectable I could have her back. . . ."

"Life is unfair." They stare at me blankly. "So is death. Your anger is ruining the lives of generations of women. I cut myself. I nearly killed my best friend. I might be locked up in an institution." I can tell I'm getting through to them. Prudence's neck looks straighter and Primrose is no longer charred; her skin is red and looks scalded instead. "You are both ruining my life!" I yell.

"As she destroyed mine," Primrose says.

"And she, mine," Prudence echoes.

They look physically identical now, but I can see that Primrose has a wild aura about her, while Prudence seems shrewder. Why can't they see how alike they are?

I think of Fiona, and it comes to me suddenly.

I step forward and place a hand on each of their shoulders. I look Prudence in the eyes. "You've tortured me and made my life a living hell, but I forgive you, for all you have done and all you have made me do and even the stuff that I think is your fault but isn't." I look into Primrose's eyes and say the same thing.

"You offer your forgiveness as if it is nothing," Prudence says.

"It should not be so freely given," Primrose chimes in. At least they finally agree on something.

"Not as if it is nothing, as if it is everything," I tell them. I am starting to get a strange feeling in my chest, and I realize it's because up until now there has been no feeling in my chest at all.

"Please," I beg. "Remember . . ." We are back in the Highlands. Two children play in the distance. "Please, forgive each other and move on. Stop torturing yourselves."

I am pulled into the sky through a black tornado.

48

ḥeatḥer

I PUKE UP water and suck in air, but it is not enough. My lungs burn and my whole body aches. I cough up more water and gasp. Someone is rubbing my back.

"I'm okay," I sputter. At least, I think I am. Sheena drapes a towel over me and I wrap it around myself, shivering.

They bring me hot tea and a change of clothes. I tell them I don't know if it worked, if it was all worth it. I hope the sisters can forgive each other and move on, and leave my family in peace.

I rest on the couch for a long while before I go home. If my aunt hasn't woken yet, she will soon. With each passing moment I feel lighter, as if a weight has been lifted.

"I think they're gone," I tell Sheena before I leave. I can't put into words the strange emptiness I feel.

She hugs me. "I hope so, love."

Janet drops me off on her way back to the hospital and asks me a million questions about the afterlife and what I saw. To be honest, I don't remember much. Only children laughing and my desperate plea.

I let myself into the apartment. I must not have locked the door when I sleepwalked up to Arthur's Seat, because the door is wide open. I go inside, hoping to go straight to my aunt's room and curl up next to her in bed, but instead I find my mother and father sitting in the kitchen. They look up at me when I walk through the door, their faces set and angry.

I am so busted.

"It was my idea," I tell them. We're at the kitchen table; I sit with my arms crossed. "I'll go back to the Wellness Center, or wherever you want me to go. . . ."

My mom's face tightens. She takes a deep breath. I know she's trying to calm down. "I'm sorry we didn't discuss the hospital with you. We would have told you."

"After you had me committed?" I mutter, not really angry. She just wants a normal, healthy daughter.

"It was never set in stone. I just wanted to find out about alternative treatment options." She takes another deep breath. "It's not easy, watching you suffer like this," she says quietly. "I just wish I could help you."

"The pills Dr. Casella gave me are actually helping a lot."

"You mean the ones on your dresser? The full bottle? The ones you clearly are not taking on a regular basis?"

Busted again.

"And this thing with Fiona . . ." She shakes her head. She doesn't know what to make of it.

"Are we going back to Chicago?" I ask. I glance at my dad. He still hasn't said anything. He just looks shocked, staring at the bandage on my arm.

That look kills me.

"I don't know what to do," my mother says.

How do I convince them I'm better? If I tell them the truth, that our family was haunted by witches and I've broken the curse, I'll definitely be locked away.

"I'll do whatever you want," I tell them. "I won't be any more trouble. I'm sorry. Don't blame Aunt Abbie. Please."

My father speaks up at last. "She's an evil genius. Getting cancer so no one can stay mad at her." It takes me a moment to realize he's joking.

I give him a half smile, which quickly drops. It's hard to find humor in Aunt Abbie's cancer.

"You'll have to earn back our trust," my mother tells me.

"I know."

"We're going to up your therapy to three times a week. Dr. Casella will be available on Skype."

"So we're staying?" I ask.

"We'll stay out here with you for a couple of weeks, then all go back together. I think our being here will be better for you."

I turn to my father but can't meet his gaze. "Sorry,

Dad . . ." Before I know what's happening, he's out of his chair and reaching for me, grabbing me into a big hug.

I'm banished to my room, where I decide to take a nap. I'm so tired, and my dreamless sleep is just what I need. By the time I wake up it's night, and I stumble out into the living room.

Aunt Abbie offers me a weak smile from her chair. She's watching the news with my dad, while my mom is reading.

"Hey," I say awkwardly.

"We went to visit your gram today and she seemed much better," my father says.

"Really?" My breath catches in my throat.

For the first time in a long time, I have hope.

The next day I'm the perfect daughter. I don't talk back to my mom. I don't get into any trouble. The only time I leave the apartment is to visit Gram with my parents. She's crystal clear, and I don't get any time alone with her to ask about the coven, but I can tell by her gaze that she knows something is up. After ten minutes of chatting with my parents, she's also figured out that Aunt Abbie isn't well.

"The cancer, it's back, isnae it?" she asks quietly.

"Mum, we didn't want to worry you. . . ."

Gram nods, asks about treatment. We promise to come back tomorrow. When we leave, I hear the nurses remark that it's strange for her to be so sharp for so long.

Back at the flat, I'm allowed to have my phone. Fiona's recovering at home. I want to call Asha . . . but I don't. The last time we spoke was too awkward.

Robby shows up on day two of my punishment. To my surprise, I'm allowed to see him. We sit in the kitchen while my parents are in the living room, pretending not to listen.

"So . . . ," Robby starts, studying the table. He looks up at me, fixes his blue eyes on my face. "What happened, really?"

I glance at my parents, keep my voice low. "I . . . it's really hard to explain," I tell him.

"Try me," he says, but I can't find the words. He reaches across the table and gently takes my hand. "I'll start. I'm really sorry about the other night. I shouldnae have called you . . . well, you know."

I shake my head. "I was acting kind of crazy."

"Still, I'm glad you didnae punch me."

"I thought about it," I admit with a small smile. I take a deep breath. "Look, Robby, I wasn't at film camp at the beginning of the summer."

"You werenae?"

I shake my head. "I was at, well, they call it a wellness center. . . ." I don't look at him as I tell him about the cutting, about the impulses. I leave out the magic and the ghosts because that's just too much to explain. "Your mom helped me out a lot. That's why I was there the other night. I'm much better now. . . ." I trail off. I don't want to see his face, his look of revulsion.

He moves closer to me, takes my chin in his hand, and makes me meet his eyes. "I'm glad you told me," he says. "If you need help, I'm here. Or if you just need a mate, I can do that too."

I swallow. "Just a mate?" I ask. He wants to be friends now, nothing more. "I guess this changes the way you feel about me." I'm on the verge of tears.

To my surprise, he laughs. "Heather. Don't be daft. I have loved you for as long as I can remember."

"You have?" I sniffle.

"And I love you now."

"You do?"

"That isnae going to change."

"It's not?" I can't seem to form coherent thoughts, only ask stupid questions.

"I'm yours, if you want me." He gives me a big hug, then kisses me, even though my face is wet from tears and I probably look like a total mess.

I hear my father yell, "Oi," from the other room and my mother shush him and say quietly, "Leave them."

I break away from Robby and smile up at him. "Um . . . I'm still grounded, I think. . . ."

"You sure are," my mom says. I roll my eyes, but I don't really mean it.

"But you can probably stay and watch some TV with us," I tell him.

"Aye," my father calls. He scoots to the middle of the couch. "You sit here, Heather." He points to his left. "And, Robby, you sit here." He pats the cushion to his right. "And I'll stay right here in the middle."

It's my mom who makes him move so Robby and I can sit next to each other. It's funny, my mom is so neurotic about me—and I guess deservedly so—but she sure loves the idea of me and Robby being together.

He stays for dinner and after, until my parents finally put their foot down. When he kisses me goodnight, it feels not like the end of the evening, but like the beginning of something else. Something good.

I haven't cut once in the past week. Gram has been lucid, and we bring her home for an overnight visit. We have dinner together as a family and my dad tells lame jokes. Gram hovers over Aunt Abbie, who looks pale and only picks at her food.

After dinner the adults sip whisky and tell stories about long ago. I've had enough of the MacNair family past to last me forever, so I just sit quietly until they go off to sleep. Gram gets her old bed, so I'm stuck on the couch, but I couldn't be happier.

Sometime in the middle of the night I wake from dreamless sleep. The flat is quiet, but something seems not quite right. I check my parents first, but they're asleep. Next, I look in on my aunt.

"Aunt Abbie?" I ask, peeking into her room.

She's sitting up in bed. The room is dark and smoky.

"Heather, love . . . ," a weak voice says, and I see that it isn't my aunt sitting up, it's my grandmother. Aunt Abbie is still in bed.

"Gram, why aren't you sleeping?" I ask.

"You beat them, didnae you?"

"Primrose and Prudence? I didn't beat them, I just made them understand they didn't have to be so angry. Gram, they've left," I tell her.

"All those years. I could have stopped them. I was so afraid of death, but you were fearless. And now what does an old woman have to fear?"

"They won't bother you anymore. No more dreams, no more visions." I am so relieved to be able to say it out loud.

"It hardly seems possible."

"But it is. I don't have the urge to cut anymore, and you're you again. It was them all along, but now that they're gone, we can be better again."

"Not all of us will be better, Heather. Your aunt's in bad shape." Her voice is so low. I take a few steps closer.

"Gram . . . what . . . ?" I notice the bowl, the smell. She has a small fire burning, her wrist dripping blood. Each splatter sizzles.

"What are you doing?" I ask, though I can see. "You said you didn't know how to do Blood Magic."

"I know enough."

"You can stop now. If you're head is clear, you have so much more life to live," I plead.

"And what? Live while my daughter dies? There isnae a mother alive who would let that happen if she had the power to stop it. Let me do this for her." She holds out her uncut arm to me. "Come, Heather. Sit with me."

And I do. I sit by my grandmother as she gives her life to her daughter.

heather

THE FUNERAL TAKES place on a Saturday.

I walk slightly away from the group, through the head-stones. The priest didn't know my grandmother, and his voice is grating.

Gram made her choice. She gave her life for her daughter. I'm sad, but it's a gentle sadness. I was with her at the end. I got to say good-bye.

I told my parents that Gram thought the horror movie I wanted to make was real. Her dementia was so far gone, my parents believed me. They told me to be thankful that Gram had her moments of lucidity at the end, that we got to speak with the real Gram one more time. They told me not to blame myself, that mental illness is to blame. It does run in our family, after all.

Aunt Abbie's cancer is in remission. My dad said something about a silver lining.

Even though my mom can check me for cuts anytime she wants, I am definitely not off the hook. When we get back home, I have to go to daily group therapy sessions and see Dr. Casella three times a week. But at least I still have a life.

I'm done with magic. The cut under my arm, the one I made after I healed all the other scars, is healing. After a while it will fade, though not completely.

I touch a stone grave marker. They're not in my head anymore. Primrose and Prudence have found peace.

"Heather." Robby's deep voice envelops me. I turn and offer him a small, sad smile.

"Everyone is headed back to your aunt's place," he tells me. I lean in and hug him.

"I'm glad you're here," I say.

He kisses the top of my head and I look up. His lips softly touch mine, gentle and comforting.

Fiona's voice interrupts our moment. "Probably not the best place to make out. You know, in the middle of a graveyard." She's been on bed rest for days, but when she found out about the funeral, she insisted on coming. She's paler than usual, but she's okay.

"Gram wouldn't mind," I tell her.

Asha and I never officially made up, but Fiona doesn't hold a grudge, so Asha has made it a point not to either. I put my arms around them.

"Thank you both for being here," I say.

"Of course." Asha smiles. "We're your friends."

Robby wraps us all in a bear hug, and despite myself, I giggle.

As we make our way up the hill to join the rest of the group, I can just make out the sound of children laughing.

The wind tickles my skin, and it smells crisp, like the Highlands.

acknowledgments

I'm so glad that I get to publish a book set in Scotland. I've been in love with Scotland since I went to university there and always jump at any excuse to head back, whether in person or through my writing. Is it weird to thank a country? Well, anyone who knows me knows I'm a bit weird, so . . . thank you, Scotland! Thank you for inspiring me with your amazing history and beautiful places, and of course, thank you for kilts.

I'd also like to thank my critique partners, Kate Karyus Quinn and Mindy McGinnis, for your insights and comments. Your words of encouragement were always appreciated. You guys are the best!

Thank you to my wonderful husband, Justin, for your

unwavering support. Your optimism may even rub off on me one day. Thank you for not judging me when I wear pajamas for three days straight, and thank you for the steady stream of coffee and snacks.

I'd also like to thank my agent, Maura Kye-Casella, for all your hard work. And thank you so much for pointing to *Bad Blood* and saying, "Yes, that's the one!" You're the best agent anyone could hope for!

Thank you to everyone at Delacorte Press. Thank you to my editorial team, Krista Vitola, Colleen Fellingham, Tamar Schwartz, and Megan Whalen. You now know all my dirty little grammar secrets . . . and that I have a mental block on when it's appropriate to capitalize *aunt*! Also thank you to Adrienne Waintraub, who works tirelessly with schools and libraries. Thank you to Ray Shappell for all your work designing a kick-ass cover.

And last but certainly not least, thank you, Wendy Loggia. I am so happy that I got to work with you on *Bad Blood*. I love that you push me to dig deep with the characters and to pull through plot threads I otherwise would have left dangling. I also love your smiley faces in the margins. They made my day so many times. I couldn't ask for a better editor.